**CA**

**Lily Wu.** A young Chi
grace and intelligence. H...

**Janice Cameron.** A native-born Hawaiian who has written a major romance novel being filmed in the islands. She is Lily's foster sister.

**Lady Blanche Carleton.** The reigning Waikiki Widow and a great beauty. Conveniently, her old, rich British diplomat husband died as they were leaving China. Inconveniently, he left his money to his sister. Fortunately, there are a lot of foolish rich men in Hawaii.

**Henry Hunter.** A tea importer, he's lost his mind and heart to Blanche.

**Jean Hunter.** Henry's loyal niece and employee. She doesn't trust Janice. She's also in need of a serious makeover.

**Hollis Knight.** An importer who shares space in a building with Henry.

**Matt Webster.** A missionary just arrived from China and in ill health.

**Tom Brittain.** Owner of Paradise Teas, he appears to be making a fool of himself over the Waikiki Widow. Appearances can be deceiving.

**Dan Gordon.** A mining engineer who shows unusual interest in Blanche during a voyage on the *Lurline*.

**Harry and Dorothy Fentriss.** Tourists who also fall into the widow's web while on the *Lurline*. Detroit will never seem the same.

**Madame Li.** A friend of Lily's family, she barely escaped China with her life after being tortured.

**Hartford Tseng.** A former palace slave, he's now a wealthy man with seven adopted daughters named for flowers—Lily's island "irregulars."

**Yao Kung.** Blanche's houseboy in China, now posing as Madame Li's servant. His dying words, "tea. . . dragon. . .tiger," puzzle Lily.

Plus **Stephanie "Steve" Dugan**, friend and reporter; **George "Gogo" Leung**, a rich playboy who admires Lily; and **"Mac" Mackenzie**, a tea-taster, as well as assorted servants, islanders, film people, tourists and members of Lily's vast extended family.

Books by Juanita Sheridan

The Lily Wu Quartet

*The Chinese Chop* (1949)
Reprinted in 2001 by
The Rue Morgue Press

*The Kahuna Killer* (1951)
Reprinted in 2002 by
The Rue Morgue Press

*The Mamo Murders* (1952)
Reprinted in 2002 by
The Rue Morgue Press

*The Waikiki Widow* (1953)
Reprinted in 2003 by
The Rue Morgue Press

with
Dorothy Dudley
*What Dark Secret?* (1943)

# *The Waikiki Widow*

**by Juanita Sheridan**

**The Rue Morgue**
**Boulder / Lyons**

*The Waikiki Widow*


ISBN: 0-915230-59-3

Reprinted with the permission of Ross Hart,
the author's son and literary executor

The Rue Morgue Press
P.O. Box 4119
Boulder, Colorado 80306
Tel: 800-699-6214
Fax: 303-823-9799

Printed by
Johnson Printing

PRINTED IN THE UNITED STATES OF AMERICA

# About Juanita Sheridan

Juanita Sheridan's life was as colorful as her mysteries. Born Juanita Lorraine Light in Oklahoma on November 15, 1906, Sheridan claimed in a lengthy letter to her editor at the Doubleday, Doran Crime Club that she came by her knack for murder naturally, since her maternal grandfather was killed by Pancho Villa in a holdup while her own father may possibly have been poisoned by a political rival.

After her father's death, Sheridan and her mother hit the road, touring the American West. When she was on vacation from boarding school, Sheridan was often put by her mother on a train "with a tag around my neck which told my name and destination. I was never afraid, and never lost."

That self-reliance came in handy years later when at the height of the Depression (ca. 1930) Sheridan, with an infant son in arms, found herself dropped off at the corner of 7th and Broadway in Los Angeles with only two suitcases and five cents to her name. She used the nickel to telephone a friend, who loaned her five dollars, and went out and got a job as a script girl for $20 a week. Her son Ross went to live with a rich Beverly Hills foster family and at about the age of six was legally adopted by his maternal grandmother. After the adoption, Sheridan, who had by then sold a couple of original screenplays, headed for Hawaii to begin her writing career. Life wasn't all that easy in Hawaii and once again she hit the pawnshops, although, as usual, "the typewriter was the last to go."

To those people, editors included, who thought her plots contained more than a touch of melodrama, Sheridan said she was only writing from life, having been clubbed by a gun, choked into unconsciousness by a man she never saw, and on two occasions "awakened from a sound sleep to find a pair of strange hands reaching for me through the dark. . ."

Sheridan, who married as many as eight times, never used much of the material she gleaned from real life, figuring that no one would believe it: "One of my most interesting friends in Hawaii was the madame of a 'house.' She looked like a schoolteacher, wore glasses and spoke New England. She had a record collection and a library. She was 26 and her annual net was higher than that of many high-voltage executives. I visited her place occasionally, and after the girls learned to trust me I heard some biographies which can't be printed—no one would believe them."

While in Hawaii, Sheridan began selling short stories. She also married architect Fritz Elliott, at which time she asked that Ross be allowed to join her in Honolulu. When the boy's grandmother—and legal guardian—refused, Sheridan came to the mainland, snatched the boy while the older woman was out for a walk and sneaked the two of them on board the *President Hoover* with the steerage passengers, "down where they eat with chopsticks at one big table, the toilets are without doors, and there is no promenade deck." Ross remembers that they embarked on the ship the very day his mother "kidnapped" him, but Sheridan claimed that she and the boy hid out in San Francisco for a week while the FBI hunted for them.

Sheridan sold several stories, including two mysteries with Asian characters, which won $500 prizes. Ross left Hawaii in May 1941 and went back to live with his grandmother. Sheridan, with the manuscript to *What Dark Secret* in her hands, left Hawaii in November of the same year, just a couple of weeks before the Japanese attack on Pearl Harbor.

At some point during this period she settled down (for the time being) in a housing cooperative on a 130-acre farm in Rockland County, New York where she and her current husband bathed in a stream and slept in a tent while helping to construct their house.

Sheridan returned to Hollywood briefly when one of her Lily Wu books was sold to television as the basis for the pilot of a mystery series set in Hawaii. She "left after a couple of sessions with the Hollywood movie types," son Ross reported, because "she couldn't stand the hypocrisy."

Eventually Sheridan settled in Guadalajara, Mexico, with her last husband, Hugh Graham, and found work as a Spanish-English translator. A fall from a horse (she learned to ride while working as a polo horse exerciser in Hollywood in the 1930s) left her with a broken hip. The last time Ross saw her she was in extreme pain and would "lock herself in her room and mix painkillers and alcohol to try to ease the pain." She died in 1974.

Her mystery writing career was brief but memorable for its depiction of mid-twentieth century Hawaii and for creating one of the earliest female Chinese-American sleuths. If Sheridan called Lily "Oriental," rather than today's accepted term, Asian, she was only using the civilized parlance of the day, just as many a modern woman will be surprised to learn that the attractive Janice wears a size 14 (those were the days, before designers went to their current flattering size system, when women yearned to be a "perfect 12"). Her books are a fierce defense of the many cultures that make up Hawaii. Unlike Sayers or Christie or countless other writers from the first half of the century, she was able to rise above the petty prejudices of her time.

For more information on Sheridan see Tom and Enid Schantz' introduction to Rue Morgue Press edition of *The Chinese Chop*.

*For May and Stephen Leeman.*
*Thanks for the Dragon Well*

# *The Waikiki Widow*

# CHAPTER ONE

I HAD BEEN AWAY from Honolulu for ten days, visiting the Farnhams at Alohilani, their ranch on the island of Maui. The climax of our house party was a luau, the ranch hands' welcoming feast for Leslie, Don's bride of six months. The next day we should have rested, but Alan Hart, who was starring in the movie being filmed from my Hawaiian novel, was due to return to Honolulu, and Don had promised to teach him spear fishing. So we were up early, and by midmorning our sampan was anchored offshore at Don's favorite fishing cove.

Leslie and I lay in bathing suits on top of the cabin while Mahoe, Don's head *paniolo,* watched the compressor which sent air to the two men below. Leslie looked out from under the arm which shielded her eyes and said, "The sun's getting hot, Janice."

"Afraid you'll burn?"

"No. This tan seems to be permanent." She moved a leg toward mine and compared colors. "But I'll never get that lovely golden shade you have. I don't see how you keep from turning red—most blondes do."

"I'm lucky," I admitted. "And don't forget I've lived in Hawaiian sun most of my life."

"Of course," she said, and dropped that subject for the one which most concerned her. She raised to her elbow and asked, "How long have they been down, Mahoe?"

The old Hawaiian sent her a reassuring smile. "Forty minutes. Pretty soon come up, I t'ink."

"They can stay under more than an hour, Leslie," I reminded her, and she received this with a nod, trying to look unconcerned.

"Are you going down again?" I asked.

"I don't think so. I've had enough for today. But I do wish—" She sat up as a dark head broke water and a masked face, like something out of science fiction fantasy, moved toward us, trailing rubber tubes. By the time Alan slipped the triangular diving mask back on his brow the second head surfaced, and soon the two were aboard. Don hauled up their string. We congratulated the men and admired the catch. Most of them were *Uu*, brilliantly colored and comically popeyed. There were a few parrot fish and one six-pound *Nohu*. Alan jumped when it flopped a spiny tail against his ankle.

"Ugh! That's a hideous thing. What did you want it for?"

Mahoe grinned. "That kin' plenty *ono*—good for eat. I t'ink mebbe we have luau tonight again."

As we headed back toward the ranch Alan said, "I couldn't stand another so soon. What music! What dancing! And the food!" He looked down at his tanned stomach as if surprised to see it still so flat.

Leslie said dreamily, her head against Don's shoulder, "It was wonderful, wasn't it?"

"Yes," Don said. "It was a fine luau. Only one thing missing—Lily."

Alan looked interested. "Is that a flower? Or something to eat?"

"Neither," I told him. "Don means Lily Wu, the girl I live with."

"Lily Wu," Alan repeated. "Chinese?"

"Yes," Leslie answered, and added, "She's Janice's foster sister."

Alan turned to me. "Were your family missionaries?" He was probably thinking of missionaries adopting abandoned girl babies in China.

"No," I told him. "My father taught at the University of Hawaii. Both my parents are dead. It was the Wus who adopted me."

"I'd like to hear about that sometime."

"Perhaps sometime I'll tell you."

"Why couldn't Lily Wu come to Leslie's party?"

"She's away for a few weeks," I said evasively, and changed the subject. "Do you still plan to do that underwater scene yourself, Alan?

Half the population of the islands wants to understudy for you."

"Wouldn't miss it for anything!" He added with emphasis, "But you could have grated carrots on my goose-pimples when that eel came out of the rocks! And when I turned to look for Don, I saw him riding toward me on a turtle big as a jeep!"

"No hands, too!" Don said, laughing.

Then Alan grew more serious and pointed to black letters on the side of the cabin. "*Molowaa*," he read. "What does that mean?"

"Lazybones," Don told him. "And you pronounce each vowel separately. You see, the Hawaiian language . . ." Alan listened and repeated the name.

While Don gave a language lesson I watched our foamy wake and withdrew to my own thoughts, which were of Lily. I hadn't told them where she was or why she hadn't come to the luau, because I did not know.

When I left Oahu we had agreed that she would follow soon. But Lily had telephoned the day after I arrived at the ranch and said that she was going away for a while. It was not like her to give the Farnhams a slight. She was as fond of them as I. She could be having a love affair, I thought, and hoped that the man wasn't George Leung, whom his local playmates call Gogo. He is amiable, indolent, and swooningly good-looking, with about as much depth as a saucer. He also has several million dollars which he would delightedly squander on Lily—the one woman in his life who consistently refuses her favors—if she would only marry him. But Lily doesn't need money, and she certainly doesn't need any more men than already clutter up the place.

This might be a new one, I thought, someone she feels serious about. Selfishly I hoped not; I don't want our partnership altered. I wondered where she had gone: to the mainland perhaps, San Francisco, or New York. At that I sighed. I was getting restless myself, ready for a trip somewhere . . .

The *Molowaa* nosed against the wharf and its motor died. As we walked up the path toward the big ranch house, Haru came out and trotted toward us.

"What is it?" Leslie asked.

The Japanese woman bobbed and smiled. "Telephone. Somebody talk you." She spoke to me.

I quickened my step. "Is it Lily?"

"No." She gestured with her hands, holding them twelve inches apart. "I t'ink big-foots lady."

"Steve!" I said, and burned into the house. Her name is Stephanie Dugan, but nobody calls her that except tourists whom she interviews for the paper. Steve wears size nines, which cause no end of amusement to her tiny-footed Oriental friends. Once at the beach she and Lily sat with their bare feet together and the contrast was so ridiculous that the three of us still laugh at the memory.

I picked up the telephone and said, "Hi, Steve. What's on your mind?"

"I'm going out to the airport this afternoon," she said. "Thought you might like to go with me. Lily's coming in."

"She is?" Lily must have gone to San Francisco, I decided, and told Steve, "I didn't get much sleep last night, and we were out fishing early. Give her my aloha and tell her I'll be home in a few days." I added, curious, "How come you're going to meet her?"

"I'm not," Steve said. "Have to interview somebody else. When I checked the passenger list of the Hong Kong clipper I saw Wu Hsui-Ming—that's Lily's Chinese name, isn't it?"

"The *what* clipper?"

"The Hong Kong clipper. Due at five this afternoon. Well, so long, Janice—"

"Wait a minute. I think I'll go along. Where can I meet you?"

"Better come to the office. I'll be working until time to start."

I agreed and hung up. Hong Kong! What on earth was Lily doing there? Over five thousand miles away, and so far as I knew she had no relatives or even close friends in that part of the world. China, yes, but no one could go to China now. Crossing that border was about as easy as making a trip to Moscow.

I went up to Leslie's room and said that I wanted to get to Honolulu in time to meet the clipper. I didn't mention Hong Kong, and Leslie took for granted that it was the California clipper I meant.

"Don't worry with luggage," she said. "Haru will pack for you while we eat."

"Pack?" Alan said, coming out of his room. I explained again. He looked pleased, and said I could fly back with him; the studio was sending transportation. Don appeared and contributed that the aquaplane would pick us up at the wharf in an hour, so we had plenty of time.

On the way back to Oahu I gave Alan another lesson in Hawaiian. He complimented me by saying I made meanings clearer than Don had done, and I explained that my father had taught the language. "Perhaps I picked up some of his method, listening."

"You must have learned discipline from him, too," Alan told me. "I've been wondering how you were able to write that book. Not that it's any work of art, of course— Sorry, Janice, I didn't mean—" He floundered into silence. When I began to laugh he was relieved.

"Go on," I said. "I lost what little vanity I had some time ago."

"It's not that you don't seem intelligent enough," he said, making an effort to be honest. "But you're young, and good-looking, and—well, I guess you seem too happy to be a writer."

"Thanks for the young and good-looking," I said. "Actually I feel younger now than I did when I began the novel. I had just lost my father then, I had an office job I loathed, and at the time I needed him most my great love jilted me for another girl. So I took it out in a book. The background is good because I learned Polynesian folklore from my father—it was his hobby. The romance probably stemmed from my own frustration. Anyhow, it turned out well. I made a lot of money and that helped me to go to New York, where I met Lily. She came back here with me, and right now we're having a very good time."

"I don't see how anybody can work in a place like this," Alan said. Then we talked about the picture and I sympathized over the lack of privacy which his life permitted, the mobs which followed him, and the clamor of local hostesses for his presence at their parties.

"Speaking of parties," he said, "we're invited to one tonight which might be fun. I wish you'd come along."

"Need a bodyguard?" I teased. He turned his incredibly handsome face toward me with a smile. "Not this time."

"Where is the party?" I asked. If it was one of Honolulu's more boring lion hunters, not even friendship for Alan would take me there.

"At the Royal Hawaiian," he told me. "I met the lady the other day, and she's quite a charmer. Has a title, too."

"You don't by any chance mean Lady Blanche Carleton? The one they call—"

"Don't stop," he said. "What do they call her?"

"They call her the Waikiki Widow."

"So she's a widow. I wondered where Sir Whatchamacallit was." He frowned slightly. "How did she get that nickname—from local gossips?"

"Yes. But it doesn't mean a thing. Ever since I can remember there has been a Waikiki Widow—it's practically a tradition here. One year there was a woman from Australia. Another time it was an ancient dryad who used to be in the Vanities. Those women generally share several attributes—they are widows, they have money, and they frolic at Waikiki."

"And what form does their frolicking take?"

"It varies. The Australian—incidentally, she looked exactly like the sheep her husband made his fortune from—adored young sailors. Our ex-Vanities queen liked the beach boys. You've met Lady Blanche—what is *she* like?"

"I really don't know, Janice, except—she's fascinating."

Alan had probably seen more beautiful women than the Aga Khan. Such comment from him meant that Lady Blanche must be really special. I had heard of her as a recent arrival in Honolulu, but did not expect that we would meet, since the Waikiki crowd was not the milieu which Lily and I preferred.

"I'd like to go to that party," I told Alan, "if I can make it. May I bring Lily along?"

"By all means. How will I know?"

"I'll call your hotel tonight around eight. Get ready for the splash—we're coming down!"

Steve and I arrived late at the airport. She stopped her car at the lei vendors' shacks so I could buy a carnation lei for Lily, and when we'd gone a few yards farther a rear tire went flat. We lost time by this and when we parked the car we saw by the crowds that the clipper had arrived. When Steve suggested that I go up to the Short Snorter bar and wait until she found Lily, I was glad to escape the heat and confusion. I ordered a drink and sat watching people, listening to snatches of conversation, and wondering again why Lily had made such a trip.

A diminutive servant girl came into the room, wearing flat slippers and trousers, long black braids dangling over her blue cotton jacket. She went to the bar and I glanced idly at her then did a double take as I recognized my foster sister. The bartender gave her a tray with a glass on it, then poured brandy into the glass. She had turned with it when I reached her and called, "Lily!"

She stopped. The reaction that first flashed in her eyes was surprise—and then resentment. She said, "Hello, Janice. I did not expect to see you here."

The pink carnation lei hung over my arm but I didn't offer it. "Steve told me you were on the clipper," I said. "When she suggested meeting you I thought it was a good idea."

She smiled then, and her eyes lit with affection. "Of course. And I thank you." She glanced at the tray in her hands. "Can you wait here for a minute?"

A stranger approached and spoke to her in Mandarin. He could have been any age from eighteen to thirty. He had a pale face and dark-circled eyes which darted around the room, returning often to Lily as if she were the one known element in a strange and wondrous world. His shabby clothes were ill-fitting and the long coat sleeves made his hands look unnaturally delicate. He asked a question, and she answered reassuringly. When he smiled he looked briefly like a very young man. Lily gestured toward me, offered him the tray, and made some kind of request. He nodded and took the tray, starting off immediately. She exclaimed, "He's going in the wrong direction!" and went in pursuit. She stopped him and then turned back to me. "I can't talk here, Janice. Are you going home now?"

"I suppose so."

"I'll come to the house as soon as I can." She went out with the young Chinese close to her side.

When Steve arrived she found me brooding into my glass, wearing a perplexed look on my face and Lily's carnations around my neck.

"Did you see her?" Steve asked.

"Yes."

Steve sent me a keen glance. "Oh. So you're not talking, either." She sat down with a grunt and lit a cigarette. "And my guy gave me the brush-off. Army hush-hush." She held up a battered white oxford and looked at it resentfully. "*Auwe!* My feet hurt!"

"Let me buy you a drink." I ordered a rum collins for her, then watched the thinning crowd while Steve drank. "Look here, Janice," she said presently, "I know there's a story in this somewhere, but if you and Lily want to keep your little mouths shut I won't insist, although the boss will give me hell if he finds out. But I warn you—" Her number-nine came down on my instep and she leaned closer and hissed, "—so, we found them there together in the teahouse, and she was wearing a gold lame gown slit to the waist while the admiral had taken off his—" She turned suddenly and said, "What do you want, Snoop? Why don't you stay on your own beat?"

Snoop was a reporter for an evening paper and he had been standing behind us. He pushed a straw hat back on a sweating head and said, "Who was wearing a gold lamé dress?"

"Yah, yah!" Steve jeered. "Go dig up your own stories, you booze hound."

His eyes narrowed, then he said, "That sidetracking don't work with me, Stevie. Come on, give—who were those people? What's wrong with the woman? What're they doing here?"

"I don't know any more than you do. I asked the servant girl if Colonel Swenton had been on the clipper with them and she didn't answer. Couldn't speak English." She stood up. "Come on, Janice. This place is too damned crowded."

Snoop followed us to the exit and rushed rudely ahead, saying over his shoulder, "Okay, Steve, I'll remember this when you want a favor." He rammed his hat down and stalked away.

"Steve," I said, "what is this all about?"

For answer she jerked my arm. "This way." We reached a side entrance in time to see a parked ambulance at the rear of which a scene was being enacted in pantomime. Two orderlies were slipping a stretcher into the big gray car. A small figure on the stretcher was completely covered by a light blanket. Near the open rear doors stood Lily. Beside her was the young Chinese.

Then we saw Snoop hurrying toward them from another direction; at sight of him Lily gave a quick command to her companion. He looked startled, then scrambled into the ambulance. Lily waited. When Snoop approached and asked her a question she looked blank and shook her head. He insisted, but she ignored him and climbed into the rear of the car. The attendant closed the doors and the ambulance drove away, leaving Snoop staring after it. He stood a moment in thought, then snapped his fingers and hurried back inside the terminal.

On the way to town Steve said, "If there's any story, Snoop will do his damnedest to see it in print."

I shrugged. "I wouldn't worry, if I were you. He doesn't know Miss Wu."

At that moment I felt annoyed with Lily. My private conclusion was that if the other reporter found out something it would serve her right. Serve her right for what? my more objective self demanded, and I remembered that I had no valid reason for resenting her lack of aloha—she had not asked me to meet her.

When Lily called, or when she came home, I would relay Steve's warning.

## CHAPTER TWO

AS IT HAPPENED, I didn't warn Lily of anything. When I saw her that evening, the first thing I perceived was that she was in no mood to talk. She came into the house quietly, still wearing the drab trousers and jacket, and for a moment she stood silent, looking around the room as if trying to reassure herself that she was back in her own atmosphere.

We live at present on Mount Tantalus, which is one of the most delightful residential sections of Honolulu. Our gate opens onto a flagstone path which curves downhill under a willow tree to the octagonal moon door. Through that door you step into an austere room with a dark, highly polished floor; the only furniture which is not Chinese is the ebony Steinway. There is a window wall which opens on a terrace from which one looks across the city to the Pacific. At the end of the terrace steps lead to a walled garden where we take most of our meals in good weather. We have two bedrooms and a kitchen. Our maid sleeps out. It is secluded and serene, and we are very particular whom we invite there.

Lily kicked off the felt slippers while she unbuttoned the frogs of the jacket. She pulled the trousers from her legs and dropped the clothes into the wastebasket. She stopped in the doorway and said, "I am very happy to be home. What is that music—*La Mer?*"

I looked up from the *k'ang.* "Yes. A new recording. There seems to be some question as to whether it is Debussy's or Toscanini's."

"It sounds tempestuous. I'd like to hear one of the *Brandenburgs* when it's finished. If you don't mind, I'll leave the bathroom door open."

She filled the tub and I began to smell geranium bath salts. After a while she came into the room wrapped in a coral crepe kimono and went to the traveling bag she had set by the door. She took out a bundle wrapped in brown paper. "I brought you something. From China, by way of Hong Kong."

When I opened it I touched folds of soft, bluish-white stuff.

Lily said, "It is *fangchou* silk. You can have a robe made of it. I'd suggest something tailored, with big pockets. As it is washed it becomes heavier and softer, and changes to cream color."

I ran my fingers over the smooth folds. "It's lovely, Lily. *Mahalo nui.*"

"You are welcome."

She sat on the floor and began to brush her hair. *La Mer* had finished and Bach was weaving cool harmonies in the room. Lily brushed for a while and then said, "There are a million and a half Chinese refugees in Hong Kong now. The congestion is incredible."

I wondered whether Lily was talking from the top of her head or was telling me something in the oblique way she sometimes uses. Possibly she implied that my *fangchou* silk had meant survival for one of those million and a half refugees.

She went on ruminatively, "It is interesting how strongly some Northern Chinese dislike the Southerners. I don't approve of their manners, but I must say I prefer their dress."

I didn't answer, just tossed a pillow to her and she lay on the floor with her long black hair spreading over the silk. Finally she said, "I couldn't talk to you at the airport today because I was escorting a friend of my family's who is very ill."

I waved a hand toward the wastebasket. "Why the masquerade?"

"The clothes were inconspicuous. No one looks twice at a servant. I wore them also out of respect to Madame Li. I am greatly indebted to her."

"Oh," I said, not understanding.

Lily explained. "Madame Li is a relative on my mother's side. You remember the years when our family was so poor—before my father recovered his business? The Lis financed my education then. They sent me to college in China, and when I wanted to return to my own country, Madame Li paid my tuition here at the University of Hawaii."

"Is she from Peking?"

"No. Hangchow. She left there recently."

"Where is she now?"

"She's at the clinic. Ethel is taking care of her."

Ethel Chun is Lily's cousin, a pediatrician who operates, in partnership with her husband, a busy clinic on Beretania Street.

"Is the sick woman going to stay here?"

"No. She's going on to New York."

Lily didn't mention the other Chinese. Since her voice sounded tired, I didn't ask more questions. After a while she said in an altered tone, "How have you been? Busy with the Hollywood people?"

"Yes. It was fun. They've finished most of the local shooting now, except some underwater scenes." I added, "You were missed at the luau. Everyone asked about you."

"It must have been a good one."

"Wonderful. And Alan Hart came for two days. He brought me back this afternoon." I looked at my watch, then started up.

"It's after eight, and I promised to call him. Alan has invited us to a party at the Royal tonight."

"A party is the last thing that I'm interested in. Besides," she sighed, "I must get back to the clinic. I want to talk to Yao."

"Yao? Is he the man who followed you to the Short Snorter room?"

"Yes. I am afraid that he is going to be a problem. I had to pull all kinds of strings to get him a visa. He was permitted to enter as her servant because of Madame Li's connections in this country. I'll tell you about that later." She sighed again.

I went to call Alan. "Sorry to be late, but I've been lazing around here and forgot the time."

"That's all right. Are you going with us tonight?"

"I'm afraid not, Alan. You'll have to face Lady Blanche without protection. Lily is tired, and I don't really feel like—" I stopped as a hand touched my wrist. "Wait just a minute." I covered the speaker and turned to Lily. "What is it?"

"Are you talking about the widow of Sir Simon Carleton, formerly of the British Legation in Shanghai?"

"I don't know where she's from. What difference does—"

"But her first name is Blanche?"

"Yes. Lily, what—"

"Tell him you'll go," she commanded. "This is very important to me, Janice. I will explain later."

I turned back to the phone. "Still there? I've changed my mind, Alan. I'd like to go."

"Fine! Shall I pick you up?"

"No. I'll meet you at the Royal. Is nine o'clock all right?"

"Swell, Janice. See you at nine."

Lily reached for the phone as I put it down. She called Ethel Chun and said, "How is she? Good. She needs to sleep. Will you give Yao a message for me? Tell him he is not to leave the building. He must be patient. I will be there soon."

She started into her room, slipping the kimono from her shoulders. "We had better dress. What are you going to wear?"

"I have a new pink cotton. How about you?"

"No cotton for me tonight. I feel in an elegant mood."

I rejected the new pink cotton in favor of lime-green crepe and went to Lily's room to see what costume her "elegant" mood had dictated.

Lily is a chameleon. She can change effortlessly into whatever character the occasion requires, and although I am accustomed to it I find this talent of hers always diverting. This time she surprised me, for I had never before seen her in the personality she assumed that night.

She had discarded the Chinese panel dress which she prefers to wear in favor of a flame-colored strapless creation which molded her figure to the waist, where it flowed in yards and yards of chiffon to her ankles. On her feet were satin platform pumps with absurdly high heels. The costume was conspicuous enough for its line and color, but she had added to it a collection of jewels which made me blink.

Around her neck was a platinum ribbon set with diamonds. Matching stones swung from her ears. I watched while she fastened glitter at her wrists, three flexible diamond bands and one of wide links set with square-cut rubies. She took out the twin bracelets which are her favorites, of jewel jade and pearls, and held them against the others.

"No," she said, "they're much too lovely." She dropped them and turned from the mirror, extending her arm.

As I fastened guard chains on the bracelets I said, "I haven't seen these before."

"Gogo gave them to me, but I've never worn them. He found out later that I prefer jade."

She rattled the bracelets and said, with a small smile, "How do I look?"

"You want the truth?"

"Of course."

"You look like a high-class tart." I stepped back a little, to see better, then shook my head. "I can't quite figure why. The jewelry is vulgar, of course, and the dress is startling, but that's not enough—it's something else—"

"It's partly this," she said, touching the black fringe which spread across her brow and changed the normally perfect oval of her face into the face of a doll. "The bangs are pinned on."

She moved into the strong overhead light of her dressing table and added, "Also, of course, the makeup."

Under that light the *maquillage* was apparent: mascara and green eyeshadow, straight-penciled, hairline eyebrows, a subtle widening and coarsening of her mouth with lip rouge.

"It's funny," I said. "You seem like a stranger."

She looked at me with a serious expression. "That might be a very good idea. Forget that we are friends unless I give you a cue to act otherwise."

"But if we're going together—"

"We aren't. I must see someone first who may be a source of information about Lady Blanche. Gogo will take me; I called him while you were dressing." She frowned slightly, then went on, "I want to meet Lady Blanche Carleton, and this can be accomplished through you and Alan Hart. After that we'll see what will happen. In the meantime let us go to the clinic. There is something I should like you to know, but first I must obtain permission to tell you."

Gogo drove us to the clinic, where we were met by Dr. Ethel Chun. Her white smock was wrinkled and she looked harassed. "I'm glad you finally arrived," she said. "I want to get home. Harry's out on a confinement and the kids have phoned twice. Richard has a Scout meeting and I promised to take Tommy to the movies."

"How is Madame Li?"

"She may be awake now. I gave her mild sedation. Take it easy with her, Lily. She began to react the moment a strange nurse walked into the room. She's a very sick woman. And that Yao—he's wandering around here poking into everything like a nosy puppy."

"I'll handle him. Go home now, Ethel, and thank you."

Ethel nodded and began to unbutton her smock. "I've left word with the switchboard that I'll be at the Waikiki Theatre," she said, and hurried out of the office.

I followed Lily down a hallway to a door where she knocked lightly and spoke in Chinese. The door was opened by Yao, who began to chatter in an excited voice. She ignored him and went to the hospital bed where a small white-haired woman lay motionless. Her eyes were closed and her face was haggard. I noticed that the covers were raised on some sort of frame at the foot of the bed.

After a moment Madame Li opened her eyes and said, "Who is this who comes with you?" She spoke in English and her voice was faint.

Lily stood near the head of the bed and motioned me to sit down. I took a chair near the high hospital table. From there I could not see the sick woman, and I understood nothing of what was said, since Lily answered her in Mandarin and their subsequent conversation was in that language. I watched Lily's expression and perceived that she was asking permission to do something, and that Madame Li refused. They argued briefly and Lily turned toward me once in a manner which suggested that she was explaining our relationship. Persuasion was useless. She finally nodded acquiescence to the older woman's will.

During this argument Yao had remained at the window. Lily turned to him. "Madame Li complains that you are restless, she is unable to sleep."

He answered in a rush of Chinese, at which she said, "I understand, Yao. But tonight you must stay here. I have not time to spend with you, and you cannot go out alone."

He looked dismayed. Lily said, "You had better be in another room, then you may move around as you wish. And perhaps we can find you a little radio. You can listen to it this evening, if you promise to tune it very low." He looked puzzled and she explained in Chinese, to which he nodded, and seemed disappointed as a child.

She rang for the night nurse and, when the girl came in, asked if there was another room available for Yao. The girl said there was one at the end of the hall, and Lily told her that he would sleep there and asked her to move the table radio from Ethel's office into his room. She said good-by then to Madame Li, who had remained silent. During this silence she had been studying me: face, hair, clothes—every movement.

I was relieved to get out of her room.

I waited while Lily and the nurse escorted Yao to the other room, and as we started toward the front of the building, told Lily I was surprised that he understood English.

"He not only understands, he can speak quite a few words. Yao learned English for his work as a houseboy. Tonight he is too nervous to talk. He has dreamed all his life of coming here—naturally he is excited. I promised him a sightseeing tour tomorrow."

I said, "Wait a minute, Lily. I feel a fit of sentimentality coming on. Do you mind if I give him this lei?" I touched the pink carnations which I had worn because they looked so lovely against the green of my frock.

Lily smiled. "There have been times when I deplored your sentimentality, but this is not one of them. Give him the lei."

I went to his door. When he opened it, I hung the flowers around his neck, saying, "Welcome to Hawaii. Giving flowers is the custom here." He gave me a shy smile and said carefully, "Thank you." He was fingering the soft flowers as I closed the door.

I hurried back to Lily and we went out to join Gogo Leung.

"Hi, beautiful doll," he said. "Where do we go now?"

"We'll drop Janice at the hotel."

"Okey-dokey."

Gogo was as near heaven as he would ever want to be, with the prospect of an evening with Lily, who was graciously wearing his diamonds. He switched on the radio and Alfred Apaka's voice came forth, singing a popular song. Gogo sang with him, off key. Under cover of the music I said to Lily, "It must have been a difficult trip for the old lady."

"How old do you think she is?"

"Oh, sixtyish, I guess."

"She is thirty-eight."

"Then—she must be very sick indeed."

"*. . .and as I gaze into your eyes . . .*" Alfred Apaka warbled.

Lily said, "She has had a frightful experience."

"What," I asked, dreading the answer, "is the matter with her feet?"

"*. . . I find myself in Paradise . . .*"

"Her feet were roasted over a charcoal fire."

I gulped, "When did this happen? And where?"

"Shortly before she left China."

"Communists?" I said automatically.

"Communists don't commit every crime in Asia, Janice."

"*When moonlight beams on my lagoon . . .*" Gogo crooned.

"Then who tortured her? Why?"

At Lily's silence I said, "She won't let you tell me anything, will she?"

"No. She is afraid. I will talk to her again tomorrow, when she has begun to feel more safe."

"In the meantime," I said, "is there anything I can do?"

"You are doing it—by arranging for me to meet Lady Blanche Carleton. We will arrive later at the Royal. Look for us."

"All right," I said, and took out my compact as we reached the hotel.

"Hi, Janice. Aloha and welcome!"

Alan stood on the lanai of the Royal, looking wonderful in his white dinner jacket, looking to me at that moment ineffably innocent with his smiling American face.

As we walked inside to join the rest of the party he said, "I'm glad you decided to come. It's going to be a good shindig."

"I'm sure it is," I said, and put a smile on my face as I summoned the mood for the Waikiki Widow's party.

## CHAPTER THREE

LADY BLANCHE CARLETON was completely unlike the woman I expected to meet. I had visualized, possibly because of her nationality and the diplomatic background, some tall, elegant creature with a veddy-veddy manner of speaking. My first thought, when she rose from our table and waited to greet us, was that the Waikiki Widow was aptly named.

To begin with, she was small. She had fine golden hair and great violet eyes, and her fair skin was so delicate that one saw the tracery of veins at her temples. Her cheekbones had the sort of hollow look which helped to make Dietrich famous, and this fragile appearance was accentuated by her light, slightly breathless voice. She had the air of a woman who has always been utterly sure of her social position but has never balanced a checkbook in her life. I made a wager with myself that her husband had been at least fifteen years her senior, and doting. Later, as I had a chance to observe her more closely, I modified that first impression of feminine softness. She was too thin, for one thing. Her neck bones were prominent, and her arms were almost as small as Lily's. If she had weighed more she might have been prettier, but, watching her during the course of the evening, I saw that she was never relaxed. Some kind of restlessness drove her. From a woman's viewpoint I found her personally interesting. I could see why Alan had called her fascinating. Perhaps many men felt that way about her.

Certainly the man beside her did. He was older than she, bald and paunchy. He rose to stand at her side. He caught her hand as he bent toward her and murmured something before giving us his attention.

Other guests watched our progress toward the table. The women in our group were either young and beautiful, or older and *soignée,* and the men were relaxed in the easy garments of success. Alan's face, of course, was known to a million fans. Lady Blanche's companion regarded us with the wide-eyed expression of a child seeing all the birthday presents which have been brought to the party *especially for him.* Our hostess greeted us with a murmur that this was delightful (for her the other hotel guests did not appear to exist) and introduced the paunchy man as her dear friend, Henry Hunter.

His name sounded familiar and I tried to recall whether I had met him before and could not. Later I remembered that the Hunters had lived in Honolulu for many years, his wife came of a missionary family, and during her lifetime he had been known as Agnes Hunter's husband.

Henry Hunter grew flushed as he was introduced to us, and the moment we were seated he signaled the waiter to start serving champagne. From his solicitousness as the wine was poured one would have thought he had pressed the grapes himself. I sat opposite Alan, between the director and a studio executive who had just flown in from California. They had hardly touched their bottoms to chairs when they began to talk shop.

The director's wife twisted a square topaz on her finger and muttered, "This is going to be a stinking dull party."

"I hope not. The food is good here. And the music."

"Food! I haven't had a square meal for twelve years. I'd get drunk, but alcohol has too many calories."

She looked at Lady Blanche, who was talking to Henry Hunter with wide blue eyes and laughter. "Now why do you suppose she invited us? More to the point—why did we come?"

I murmured something and looked around for the reason why I had come, but she hadn't arrived yet. The music started and Alan signaled me and I rose. Lady Blanche and Henry Hunter walked ahead of us. He danced awkwardly, while she smiled up at him as if she were having the most wonderful time. Why? I wondered, and tried to act as unconcerned as she was over the stares which followed our movements.

We finished a foxtrot and swung into a slow rhumba. Alan danced as superbly as he swam or rode horseback or fenced or did the innumerable other things he had been trained to do, and I was enjoying myself when he stumbled and said absently, "Excuse me," his eyes fixed on something over my shoulder. When our rhythm matched again, I turned to see what he had been watching. A few feet away Gogo Leung and Lily, with the rapt, semi-hypnotic look of *aficionados,* were maneuvering through a complicated series of steps. They finished near us and I waited. Lily met my eyes, sent me a brilliant smile, and said, "Hiya, Janice? How's your party?"

"Delightful!" I said, gulping just a little.

Alan asked, very much interested, "This isn't by any chance the Chinese Lily you told me about?"

"It most certainly is," she answered for me. "And this is my boyfriend, Gogo Leung."

Gogo almost burst his cummerbund at that title. He grinned and gave Alan a hearty handshake, and the four of us moved off the floor. Lily and Gogo were sitting with another Chinese couple at the table next to ours, and she waved good-by and dimpled at Alan as Gogo pulled out her chair.

The director said the moment I sat down, "Who is that exquisite creature?"

"A friend of mine. Would you like to meet her?"

For answer he rose to his feet, and I took him over to Lily. The next thing that happened was that he came back with the two couples in tow, and, without asking permission of our hostess, ordered a waiter to bring chairs and squeeze them into places at our table. He was the sort who didn't bother with manners, and in this new personality Lily chose to ignore them. The moribund party began to spark, and studio talk was forgotten.

The Chinese girl who was with Lily had short, permanently waved hair and a pretty face with a petted-child expression. She wore many jewels and a watermelon-pink frock which was one of a dozen Schiaparelli had made for her that summer—"When Papa took me to Paris." Her escort was Gogo Leung's prototype. They were enormously successful with the Hollywood crowd. More champagne was poured, the men danced with Lady Blanche, with Lily and Betty Chang, and dutifully partnered the rest of us ordinary women.

It was much later when Lily, whom I had been watching for some kind of communication, finally glanced at me with a flicker of her brows. When she started to the powder room I followed. We found a place at the end of the crowded dressing table, and as we faced each other in the mirror she whispered, "Try to get acquainted with Henry Hunter."

I had no chance to comment because Lady Blanche entered then with Betty Chang. Betty was saying in a petulant voice, "—all our furniture and rugs and Papa's jade collection and my new Rolls. I suppose we'll never see them again. Mama and I certainly won't go back to China now." She pursed her mouth and traced its outline with red. As she slipped the lipstick into her gold evening bag she asked Lady Blanche, "When did you leave Shanghai?"

The blonde woman said, "Simon brought me to Hong Kong just before the communists took over. He kept going back, you know, from time to time. Then we were ordered home—" She moved a white shoulder and sighed as she leaned toward the mirror.

Betty was apparently not the sensitive type. "What happened to your husband?"

The blue eyes widened at her. "He died suddenly, just before we sailed. That's why I'm staying on here for a while. The doctor advised a rest in this climate before returning to England."

"Your husband died just before you left?" Lily said. "How sad." She smoothed her black fringe with a tiny gold pocket comb.

When we returned to the table Alan asked Lady Blanche for a dance, and I looked pointedly at Henry Hunter. He jumped up and said, "Of course, of course," and away we went. He danced stiffly, with awkward little off-tempo bounces. His shoulders jerked in attempt to achieve the rhythm which his feet could not. When the music stopped he applauded, while his eyes searched the floor for Lady Blanche. Finding me watching him, he began to make polite conversation.

As he wiped perspiration from his face he said, "So you're the author of this picture they're making! I never expected an author to be so young and charming. What is the name of the movie?"

I didn't attempt to explain the difference between a screen treatment and a novel. The subject was too depressing, and he wasn't really interested. I said, "Your guess is as good as mine, Mr. Hunter. *Peril in Paradise, Polynesian Passion, Terror in the Tropics*—it may be any of those. Whatever they decide doesn't make much difference."

"But where did you learn so much about the islands? Are you a Honolulu girl?"

I told him about my father's position at the university and our interest in Hawaiiana. I said, "Your name sounds familiar. Haven't we met somewhere before?"

His face became graver. "I don't think so. You probably met my wife, Agnes."

When he spoke her name a picture of Agnes Hunter flashed into memory then, as she had appeared once at a faculty meeting to protest the university's annual beauty contest. What I remembered chiefly was how her long oily nose had twitched as she declared to blank-faced faculty members that such a disgusting exhibition of female nakedness was disastrous for student morale and had no place in an institution of higher learning.

I said, "Your wife was rather a serious person, wasn't she?"

The bald head nodded. "Never knew how to enjoy life—had it all prayed out of her when she was young. Never wanted anyone else to enjoy life either." He looked slightly startled at his own disloyalty, then relieved as music began and eliminated the necessity of saying more.

But once the first admission was made, a second seemed to come easier. "Do you know," he puffed into my ear as we jerked around a turn, "I've lived here for twenty-two years and this is the first time I've ever danced at this hotel?"

"You've been missing a lot," I told him.

"I know it," he said simply.

The music stopped again, and we started off the floor just as the moon rose over Diamond Head and shone on water which quivered beyond the terrace. At our table Lady Blanche had joined the director and Lily's Chinese friends. Seeing this, Henry Hunter offered no resistance when I suggested that we look at the Pacific. Waves washed toward us with sighing sounds, palms whispered, and in the warm night air the fragrance of many flowers mingled with the faint oceany tang.

We stood quietly. Then Henry Hunter said, "It's hard to believe, that's all, hard to believe."

"What is hard to believe?"

"Me. What's happening to me." He waved both hands. "Me, in

this wonderful atmosphere, sitting with movie stars, with beautiful women, dancing, drinking champagne—"

"This hotel has been here for a long time. The kind of people we're with arrive every day. Waikiki is their playground. What have you been doing in Honolulu all these twenty-two years?"

"I've been working," he said. "In the office during the day—I'm manager of Paradise Teas—and then, oh, I don't know—in my garden at home, playing bridge, having dull evenings with dull people. Agnes and I went to church one night each week, and twice on Sundays."

He offered a cigarette and lit it for me, then took one for himself, exhaling with satisfaction. "Never smoked before," he said. "I like it. Never tasted anything stronger than root beer, either. I like liquor, too, like it a lot, just as I like everything else I never did before." He added, so low that I barely caught the words, "Like—that word's not nearly strong enough."

"You're fortunate," I said, "to have a charming person like Lady Blanche as a teacher."

He looked at me with a grateful smile. "I certainly am. Isn't she wonderful? I never knew a woman—" He stopped.

"How did you happen to meet her?"

"In the most ordinary way. She hadn't been in Honolulu long and was driving around town one day when she passed my office. On impulse she stopped her taxi and came in—she didn't know that we're just a wholesale firm—to ask if we could sell her some Moyune—that's one of the better Chinese green teas—almost impossible to get now—which happens to be her favorite. We don't stock it, but I told her that I'd try to find some. I did, and delivered it in person. She invited me for cocktails a few days later, and then . . ." his voice faded as he remembered things he did not wish to talk about.

On the beach not far from us a young couple were strolling. They stopped and faced the ocean for a moment, then the man's arm went around the girl and his face bent to hers. After they kissed he said something in a low tone and they both laughed, the tender, secret laugh of lovers. At my side Henry Hunter drew in a sharp breath. "We'd better go back," he said.

He forgot me as soon as the blue eyes of Blanche Carleton turned toward him and she made a little gesture of welcome. When we reached her she announced, "Miss Chang has just been telling us of an interesting place which tourists never see. She has offered to take us there."

"Place?" he said. "What sort of place?"

"It's a gambling house."

"Not a public house," Betty Chang said. "Just some people we know who have a private club."

"Gambling?" Henry Hunter frowned.

Blanche's hand touched his wrist. "Do you disapprove, Henry?"

At her touch he started. "No. No, of course not. But we're having such a wonderful party—"

A thin shoulder shrugged as she said, "We can dance every night. This is something new. All kinds of gambling—roulette, dice—"

"—and fan-tan, mah-jongg—Chinese games, too," Betty Chang added.

I had moved near Blanche Carleton and my arm brushed hers. I wondered if I knew then why Henry Hunter had started at her touch. Her skin burned. Her eyes were bright as if with fever. While Betty Chang went on talking about this private gambling club, I watched Blanche pick up a glass of champagne and touch it to her mouth as if to relieve its dryness.

No wonder she was thin. She seemed to be consumed by some inner fire—and it was no hard, gemlike flame, either. Gambling fever? Possibly. She smiled at Henry and murmured something which I could not hear. He turned a long, intense look on her, and in that interchange I perceived that whatever might be the fire that burned in the Waikiki Widow, Henry Hunter was moving, with open eyes and willing feet, directly into it.

One other incident occurred before we left the hotel. We were discussing transportation while Henry Hunter and Lady Blanche waited for the check. During this interlude a girl appeared at our table, followed at some distance by her escort. I didn't notice her particularly except to note that she was quite tall, with short dark hair and a face which seemed unusually pale. She went directly to Henry Hunter and spoke in a low voice. He answered irritably, then said something to Lady Blanche, who regarded the girl with surprise and gave what looked like a reluctant invitation to join us. The girl sat down on the nearest chair, her back rigid, in an attitude of waiting.

At that point my attention was diverted by Lily. "Let's go powder our noses, Janice." I followed her little red satin feet toward the powder room.

A group of women came out as we entered, leaving the place temporarily empty. As soon as the door was closed, Lily said, "I want to show you something." She went to a chair in the corner and took a folded newspaper from behind it. "I found this here, where someone had discarded it."

When I unfolded the newspaper I saw that it was the evening sheet for which Scoop worked. Lily laid a finger on a front-page story and I read it through quickly.

WIFE OF MISSING CHINESE AGRICULTURALIST ARRIVES TODAY BY CLIPPER FROM HONG KONG

Madame Li Tsui-Yi, wife of eminent Chinese agriculturalist and educator, Li Tze-Kai, arrived in Honolulu today aboard the Hong Kong clipper, for an indefinite stay in the islands. She was accompanied by two attendants, Wu Hsui-Ming and Yao Kung, and was taken by ambulance to the Chun Clinic on Beretania Street.

Madame Li was not available for an interview, due to illness, but her presence here raises new questions concerning the whereabouts of her husband, whose last known address was in care of the National Agricultural Research Bureau at Peipei. Professor Li had accepted a post at the University of Hawaii for the scholastic year beginning in the fall of 1950, but failed to appear or notify the university of his intention to remain in China. Neither he nor any member of his family has been heard from until the arrival of Madame Li today.

A native of Chekiang, born in 1902, Li Tze-Kai received his M.S. at Michigan College of Agriculture in 1921, studied at Cornell in 1922-23, was professor of agriculture at University of Nanking, 1932-37, after which he taught at Cornell until 1946, when he returned to China to join the staff of the Agricultural Research Bureau. His friends here and on the mainland will be interested to know that his wife is on American soil, and will no doubt be able to solve the mystery of her husband's whereabouts as soon as she has recovered sufficiently to permit an interview.

I handed the paper to Lily. "This reads like an obituary."

"Yes," she said. "It came from the newspaper obituary file. The reporter doesn't know it, but the impression he gives is correct."

"Professor Li is dead?"

"He was tortured more severely than his wife."

"My God!" I gasped. "Lily, it's too awful to—"

"Don't start that!" she said sharply. "We can't alter what has already happened. But we can help Li's wife." She tossed the paper aside.

"I want to call the clinic," she said. "Let's find a telephone."

I waited while she made the call. Lily turned from the phone with a blank expression which made her look more like a doll than ever. But her voice was agitated as she said, hurrying at the same time back toward our table, "Something has happened. I must go there immediately."

"I'll go with you."

"Yes, but— I know how we can manage it, if you can get away from Alan Hart."

Alan solved that problem by saying frankly that he would much prefer bed to spending the night in a gambling house. I told him it didn't matter; I would go on with Lily and her crowd. In the meantime Lily spoke to Betty Chang, who said sure, why not, and announced that everybody was to follow her car. When we started out, Lily steered Gogo Leung toward a taxi and gave him instructions to wait for us at Lau Yee Chai's restaurant.

We took Gogo's roadster. As soon as we started I asked, "What is it, Lily?"

"Yao has disappeared."

Lily had hoped to keep the arrival of the little group a secret. I said, "If anything has gone wrong I'll feel at fault. Steve warned me about that reporter and I meant to pass it on to you. I forgot."

She was driving very fast, and she answered without taking her eyes from the road. "Nonsense. I knew he was a reporter. If anyone is to blame it is myself, for leaving them the way I did. But I had to meet that woman from Shanghai, and the party was such an excellent means—" She turned onto Beretania Street with a squeal of tires, and we didn't say anything more.

## CHAPTER FOUR

MISS CHING, the nurse who was on night duty, met us at the door. "Miss Wu, he hasn't come back yet. I'm so glad you called. I didn't know what to do."

"How is Madame Li?"

"Sound asleep."

"You are certain?"

"I just checked her pulse. She didn't even move."

"How long has Yao been gone?"

Miss Ching looked at her watch. "An hour and twenty minutes. The telephone call came at ten-fifteen."

Lily said, "Yao received a telephone call? Please tell us about it. Go slowly and try to remember everything that happened this evening after we left."

"Nothing happened, except the phone call."

"Who called him?"

"I don't know. It was a woman. She just asked for Yao."

"Did she speak English?"

"Yes. But Yao answered in Chinese."

"What did he say to her?"

"I don't know. I speak Cantonese."

"He speaks Mandarin," Lily said absently. "How did he react during the conversation?"

"I didn't watch him. While he was talking I went into Doctor Ethel's office to leave a memo about another call."

"Another call? What was that?"

The nurse had been looking at Lily's dress, jewels, and satin sandals with a wistfulness tinged with envy. At the last question she drew herself into dignity. "It was a professional matter."

Lily smiled. "I am Ethel's cousin, Miss Ching. She will not object to your telling me."

The girl hesitated, then said, "The call was from Captain Dodd's wife. Their child has had otitis media and she reported that his fever was down and he wanted food. I relayed Doctor Ethel's instructions, that he could have six ounces of fruit juice every hour. Yao's call came right after that."

"How did he act when he hung up the phone?"

"Rather surprised, I thought, and maybe pleased. I went to Madame Li's room then for her hourly checkup, and when I came back he was gone. I thought at first he was in bed, but when I looked in his room it was empty."

"The woman who called him," Lily persisted, "did she by chance sound slightly British?"

The girl moved to the edge of her chair, and her voice rose. "I don't know! She didn't say a thing to me. She asked for him."

"Please do not worry about this, Miss Ching," Lily soothed. "It is not your fault that he went out. We are just trying to find where he may have gone, since the city was strange to him. Are you sure that is all you can tell us?"

The girl added then, "When the woman was speaking, I heard music."

"What kind?"

"Dance music. I think it was some island song."

That could have been anything: radio, jukebox, or live orchestra.

Lily was starting to speak again when we heard voices at the screened door. "Open it, Sonny—*wikiwiki!*"

"Mebbe we ring a bell first?"

"No ring hospital bell. Open da door!"

By the time we three were on our feet the door was opened by a teenaged Hawaiian boy who stood holding it wide. His young face looked frightened. After him came another Hawaiian, a big man in soiled cotton *mokus*, his bright-flowered aloha shirt stained with sweat. He entered sideways, carrying a slight figure in dark clothes. A few bruised pink petals clung to the black coat and his head lolled. When the big Hawaiian was through the door we saw that the body he carried was that of Yao.

"He's hurt. Bad, I t'ink. We found him on da road."

Miss Ching said quickly, "Here, down this hall. Follow me!"

When Yao was laid on his bed, Lily said, "Call Ethel." The nurse nodded and darted out. The two Hawaiians stood slightly away from the bed, their expressions solemn.

Lily said, "Where did you find him?"

"Out near da Blow Hole."

That was miles from Beretania Street, on the road which goes around the island.

Lily bent over Yao. His face was bruised and cut, his eyes were closed, and from his sagging mouth a line of blood trickled. She looked at the big Hawaiian. "Did he ask you to bring him here?"

"No. Our kids come to Doctor Ethel—"

A few minutes later Ethel arrived, carrying her bag, saying briskly, "You men wait outside, please." They left the room.

When she opened Yao's coat we saw on his white shirt the imprint of an automobile tire. Carnation petals had been mashed onto the fabric.

"He's been run over!" Ethel bent toward him and after a while looked at Lily with a slow shake of her head.

"Can he talk?"

"Probably not. His chest is crushed."

Lily moved to the bed. "If he could tell us— *Ethel!*" For Yao's eyelids were twitching, and as we watched, his eyes opened and he looked into Lily's face.

She said softly, "Yao! You are badly hurt."

He looked at her and made an effort to speak. Blood dribbled from his mouth, but no intelligible sound came. Lily leaned closer to him. "Yao. We want to know who did this. You promised to talk to me in the morning, remember? But now you are going to be too sick to talk for a while."

His eyes fixed on hers with a wide, imploring stare. His fingers made scratching motions on the white sheet.

"He wants to write," Lily said, and looked around the room. There was nothing that Yao could write with. Lily bent over him then and raised his hand in hers. She took his index finger and touched it to the inside of her arm.

"Tell me," she commanded. "Write it here."

To Ethel she whispered, "This won't hurt him, will it?"

"Nothing more can hurt him," Ethel said.

Yao's finger moved and she watched intently, and then said, "Tea? Yes, I know it is in tea, you told me that much. Who hurt you?" She touched his hand again and once more he made a Chinese character on her flesh.

Lily frowned, concentrating. "Tiger? I don't understand."

As his fingers again went through the motions of writing a character, she said, "Tea? Yes, you told about the tea. But what kind?" He made another complicated series of motions and his hand dropped limp to the sheet. Lily bent over Yao, saying, "Dragon, Dragon what? Can you tell me more?"

But Yao told nothing more.

When we went to the reception room again the two Hawaiians were not there. Miss Ching, tears on her flat-cheeked young face, said that they were waiting outside, and Lily and I went to talk with them.

Ethel was at her desk. As we started out she called, "I must notify the police, Lily."

Lily said over her shoulder, "Of course."

We found the Hawaiians in a small truck, the rear of which was crowded with sober-faced adults and several sleeping children. The big Hawaiian climbed out of the front seat and began in a lowered voice to tell us what had happened.

They had been visiting friends at Kaaawa, combining a day's fishing with a family picnic. Since the night was warm and they were in no hurry to get home, they came around Koko Head toward the city. One of the women had made a lei which she wanted to leave on the statue which stands near the Blow Hole to commemorate fishermen who have lost their lives on that dangerous section of coast. They walked out to the statue and were looking at the moonlit sea when they saw Yao lying below them, on rocks which would soon be covered by the rising tide. They picked him up and brought him to the clinic.

"What do you think happened out there at the Blow Hole?" I asked.

"I dunno. Hit-run driver, mebbe. Sees da man's hurt bad, gets scare, toss him into da sea. Little more time da tide take him away, nobody ever fin' him."

Ethel came out and asked if they would stay until police arrived to hear their story. Lily and I thanked the Hawaiians and returned to the clinic with her. Lily said, "Is Madame Li awake?"

"No. She will sleep through the night."

"Where can I wash?" Lily held out her arm, and diamonds glittered against a smear of blood on her flesh.

"In here." Ethel pointed to a white-tiled lavatory which adjoined her office.

While Lily scrubbed she said, "If Li Tsui-Yi awakens don't let her hear about this. I'll tell her myself. She has plane reservations for tomorrow. Do you think she can travel?"

"Ask me tomorrow, after we've given her a checkup. I want Harry to look at her too. Does she have to leave immediately?"

"It will be a relief to all of us when she is safe with my family in New York."

"How about the police?" Ethel asked.

"Tell them this: Yao was a servant of the Li family. He was told not to go out alone, since he was not acquainted with the city. He disobeyed and was brought back here exactly as it happened. He probably went for a walk and may have been hit anywhere in the city, perhaps even a few blocks from here. It looks as if the person who ran over him panicked and tried to hide what he had done by throwing his body into the sea at a point where the tide would carry it away."

Ethel's eyes were fixed on Lily. "How about that telephone call?"

Lily met her gaze. "You can say that it was I who telephoned Yao, to inquire about Madame Li. My call had nothing to do with his accident, except that it may have made him restless."

Ethel looked at her cousin for a moment, then said quietly, "Of course, Lily. I'll remind Mildred Ching of that."

"Perhaps she would like to make the trip to New York with your patient."

Ethel nodded. "She will be thrilled. Mildred's never been off the island."

"I'll arrange it," Lily said. "Now, we must rejoin our party."

I followed her out to the yellow roadster and we started in silence. When the car was moving again I took deep breaths of soft night air, grateful for it after the warm rooms of the clinic, after Yao's room where the smell of fresh blood had mingled sickeningly with the fragrance of crushed carnations. Lily drove slowly toward Waikiki and Lau Yee Chai's, and I leaned back and looked up at clouds, dazzling white in moonlight, at trees which made patterns of lacy shade when we drove beneath them.

After a few blocks I lit cigarettes for both of us and then I asked, "Lily, you don't really intend to go back to that party?"

"Yes."

I said, my voice sharp, "You may want to go, but I certainly won't. I've had enough for tonight."

She stopped the car with a scrape of tires against the curb. She turned to me and said in a voice almost as sharp as my own, "You know me too well to make such an insulting remark. This affair is important, to me personally because of my relationship to the Li family, but also because it involves the welfare of many people."

I didn't answer.

Lily said, "You feel baffled, since I have not made adequate explanations. You know that I would have done so, if I had been permitted." She tossed her cigarette away and then said, "We have not the time. Also I cannot tell you all of this story. But you have a right to know part of it, at least.

"You know that I went to Hong Kong to bring back Madame Li because she was too ill to travel alone. She had escaped from China a short while ago and wrote to my family in New York. They forwarded her letter to me here, and I received it after you went to Maui."

"So you flew to Hong Kong."

"Yes. I found her ill and alone. She had almost no money left. I obtained temporary medical attention and arranged for passage on the next clipper. She was living in a very crowded place—I mentioned the number of refugees in Hong Kong now—and they were desperate—for jobs, for food, for any means of keeping alive. Under such conditions one has few secrets. Word got around that we were leaving. That was when Yao came to me. I'm telling it badly, Janice. We have no time and I am tired."

"Go ahead. I'll try to make sense out of it."

"Yao asked me to help him. He had wanted all his life to get to America. I told him it was impossible. He said then that he would make a bargain with me. He knew the whereabouts of the fortune the Lis had lost—"

"What fortune?"

"I cannot give details without permission. The Li family was bringing about half a million dollars out of China. That was why they were tortured."

"It was stolen from them?"

"Not exactly. But Yao knew what happened to it. He said that if we would bring him to the United States and help him find work he would tell us where— I had better start, Janice, it is growing late." She started the motor and continued hurriedly, "I am certain that Lady Blanche Carleton is connected with this. Yao was her houseboy. He hinted that the smuggling was being done in shipments of tea. That is why I want to know her, and why Henry Hunter has become important."

"Oh," I said. "He's manager of a tea importing firm."

We were on Kalakaua Avenue, garish with neon, heavily trafficked. Lily said, "Yao had promised to tell me everything in the morning. I should have talked to him tonight, but this chance came to meet Blanche Carleton, to study her in a situation which I have gone to some trouble to arrange. I had to make the choice, and because of that choice I have lost the chance to find out from Yao what I needed very much to know. All he told me before he died was three words: Tiger. Tea. Dragon. They are almost unintelligible. Except the tea. Blanche Carleton and Henry Hunter are concerned with tea. I am now concerned with them."

"Yao," I repeated. "I don't think I could be much help to you tonight, Lily. I keep remembering him, with my flowers—"

She looked straight ahead and said in a remote voice, "If you feel so shaken you need not force yourself to go on with this. I will drop you when I pick up Gogo. You can take a taxi home. Then, when you are home, you can spend the rest of the night remembering Yao. You can pace the floor and wring your hands and be as completely ineffectual as you wish. I have more important things to do."

Before I could answer she had stopped the car in front of Lau Yee Chai's, and Gogo Leung was hurrying toward us. "I thought you were lost, doll!" At sight of our faces he said anxiously, "Is anything wrong?"

"A little bit of trouble," Lily told him. "I will explain later. First, will you call a taxi for Janice?"

I said, "Don't call a taxi. I'm going on with you."

Lily didn't react. She merely slid over to make room for Gogo at the wheel, and we started toward downtown Honolulu. She switched on the radio, and as soon as music blared from it she said, turning her face to my ear, "When we see Henry Hunter again, I hope you can make some kind of impression on him. I will concentrate on the woman."

I said, thinking aloud, "Mr. Hunter seemed slightly impressed with meeting an author. How would it be if I told him—" I stopped, waiting for the idea.

"That you're writing a novel about tea—"

"Yes, that's it. The tea trade is exotic, has a romantic history—the old China Clippers, the tea races . . ."

Lily nodded. She said softly, "I hoped that you would come."

"I'm not sure that I—"

"Yes, you can," she said. "Put everything else from your mind. Don't permit yourself to think of Madame Li or Yao. Not for an instant:"

Torture and murder. Draw a shutter, blank them out, no matter how close they come. "All right," I said. "They're out of my mind. For now."

## CHAPTER FIVE

ING'S PLACE WAS deep in a valley which Honolulu considers an "exclusive" residential district. We followed a winding drive over several acres of garden and stopped under the porte-cochere of a big white house, where we were met by its owner, a dapper little Chinese with sharp eyes behind horn-rimmed glasses. His wife stood at his side. She was short and fat and wore a tubular, tight-fitting maroon dress and some very fine jade.

Mr. Ing trotted toward us, smiling widely, saying, "You are with the Chang party? Oh yes. We have been expecting you. Welcome."

Mrs. Ing appraised Lily's jewels and my clothes, then said to Gogo. "We have not seen you for a while." She added a phrase of crackling Chinese to which he shrugged and said amiably, "I'm a busy man, you know. Don't bother with us—I'll show the girls around."

I needed to be led, for I was dazed, first from what I had so recently witnessed, and now from such a change in atmosphere. I had never heard of this establishment. Perhaps it was new. More likely it had been here for a long time and I had not previously met the kind of people who knew about it.

A door on the right of the wide entrance hall led to three rooms lighted by crystal chandeliers and connected by arches which substituted for former wall partitions, the center of each was filled with gaming tables, while along the walls were a few sofas and chairs. We strolled in search of familiar faces. A good percentage of the guests were Oriental. From a side room came the rattle of mah-jongg tiles and a woman shrilled a Green Dragon Pung. The chuck-a-luck cage flashed as it turned, while at a round table in a corner five men sat intent on a game of stud poker.

Lady Blanche was playing roulette, flanked by a studio executive and the director. The latter's wife had given up the struggle against calories and was standing behind his chair with a highball in her hand. She saw us and crossed the floor. "We wondered what happened to you."

"Flat tire," I said.

Lily looked up at Gogo. "Shall we try some roulette?"

The director's wife said, "Roulette bores me. It generally bores The Great Man too, but—" She sent a hard look across the room. "The Waikiki Widow's having a run of luck." She shrugged. "How about a drink?"

I agreed. I had not Lily's talent for assuming the color of whatever background I happened to be in. My hands were cold; my insides felt tied in knots. We started across the hall to the bar.

"Where's Mr. Hunter?" I asked.

"He's around somewhere. Poor old guy, he isn't having much fun. He doesn't understand roulette, and when the Widow begins to win she gets tired of teaching him. Then that gloomy niece of his tags along and gives him hell about something."

"What niece?"

"Her name is Jean, and she doesn't approve of these goings on at all. She turned up just before we left the Royal—remember? A bean-pole with a sour puss. Here we are. Ghastly, isn't it?"

The bar was in a small ugly room furnished with a couple of metal tables and chromium chairs. There were five barstools, and on one of these Henry Hunter was sitting with his back to the barman, holding a glass and scowling at his niece.

I had not paid much attention to her at the hotel. In this harsh light I could see what she really looked like. Jean Hunter was not a bean-pole. She had, actually, the kind of figure a professional model prays for: tall, with narrow waist and hips and long slim legs. She could have worn almost anything with grace. But she was dressed in a blouse of some hideous calico print and a dirndl cotton skirt. Her dark, hair was cut short. Her features, without makeup, looked negligible above calico. When I studied her face I saw that she had that Greek boy look which had been so popular in Greenwich Village where I lived there a few years ago. It was out of place here.

The man who stood by her side was exactly her height. He had brown eyes and sleek brown hair and a mustache of the same color. He wore beige silk gabardine and brown-and-white sports shoes. He seemed embarrassed. As we approached he touched her elbow and said, "Come on, Jean. We'd better go." She turned quickly, about to make a reply. When she saw us she said nothing.

Her uncle greeted our arrival with relief. "Welcome, ladies! Can I buy you a drink?"

The director's wife took the stool next to his and set down her empty glass. "That's a kind offer. I accept."

The girl was looking at us with resentment and disdain. I pretended not to be aware of this and took the other stool, saying, "I'd like Canadian Club and water, please."

"Double scotch for me."

Henry Hunter's cheeks were flushed and his voice had the faintest betraying thickness. After giving our order he said, being carefully polite, "I should like you to meet my niece, Jean. And this gentleman is Hollis Knight."

Since he had not mentioned our names I added that information, smiling, wishing they would go away. Jean Hunter responded with a nod. Hollis Knight said, "Very glad to know you."

I asked, perfunctorily, "Won't you join us?"

"No, thank you," she said. Then, urgently, "Uncle Henry—"

Uncle Henry pretended not to hear. "Here's your drink," he reminded me, and turned to the bar, being host. Without glancing behind us I was aware that Jean Hunter was on the verge of admitting defeat to whatever purpose had brought her here. Hollis Knight was urging, "Come on. Jean. It's getting late." He added something in an undertone.

"But, Hollis, I told you—" She lowered her voice. Then, as emotion sharpened her tone, I caught "—a shipment due in soon. And you know as well as I do that he won't be able to—"

"Jean!" her uncle said, "Go home."

The girl gave him one last furious look and allowed Hollis Knight to lead her out of the room.

Henry Hunter sighed deeply, then seemed about to settle into a brooding silence. I said, nodding toward the director's wife, "We must watch her. She's drinking doubles."

He scowled. "Let her enjoy herself. Too many people try to stop other people from having fun. What if she does have a headache tomorrow?" He was on the verge of truculence.

I said, "It's not tomorrow's headache I'm concerned about. She's liable to fall flat on her face."

"Oh," he said, and looked worried.

We three were the only customers in the room. Now was my chance to talk to him. I suggested, "Why don't we move to comfortable seats?"

He said eagerly, "Of course. Of course. Wonderful idea!"

I slid off the stool and carried my drink toward some chairs in the corner, saying, "This will be better, won't—" then discovered that I was talking to myself. Henry Hunter was guiding the other woman into the gambling room. I followed them to a sofa directly opposite the roulette table.

"This is much better, isn't—" I tried again, and might as well have spoken to the furniture. Henry was staring at Blanche Carleton.

He sat hunched forward, and his face locked looked tired and old. He put a hand to his mouth in a sort of shielding gesture, frowned at his glass, then took a gulp which he held as if he were about to gargle.

I had to make some kind of contact with him, "Mr. Hunter."

"Eh?" He started and swallowed and coughed.

"Don't you feel well?"

He slid back an the sofa, raised his hand toward his mouth again, then reached into his pocket for cigarettes instead.

"Toothache," he told me. "Just had a new crown put on, and the blamed thing is sensitive." We were sitting under a bright light and he reached up and turned it out.

"That's thoughtful of you," I said. "Those lights are unkind to a lady at this hour."

"Nonsense, my dear," he retorted gallantly. "It will be twenty years before you have to worry over anything like that."

"I hope you're right," I said. We coquetted for a while. During this interchange he forgot his aching mouth and smiled. I saw then that what was bothering him was a new upper denture. Probably one of the lost teeth had had a gold crown, for on the right incisor of the false set was a flash of gold.

Coquetry was uphill work for both of us. Finally he lapsed into his depressed mood and frowned at his highball. I said, in an effort to reach him, "Your niece seems to be unhappy about something."

He nodded. "Jean's a worrier. She lost her parents when she was twelve, and came to live with us, and our house was never—She's too serious for her age. And since my wife died—she's tried to take over—"

"I heard her say there is a shipment arriving soon. Does that mean a shipment of tea?"

He nodded, not interested.

"Where is it coming from?"

"India. This is Darjeeling tea. Very popular."

"India!" I exclaimed. "Mr. Hunter, I think you have one of the most romantic occupations I've ever heard of!" I leaned past him to ask the director's wife, "Don't you agree?"

She jerked. She said automatically, "India. Snakes. Hot as hell. Starving people. Don't want to go there."

I turned back to Henry Hunter. "What part of India does Darjeeling come from?"

"The Himalaya Mountains. It is climate which makes the flavor of tea. Darjeeling is grown at elevations from 2500 to 6500 feet. I was there on a buying trip two years ago. Cool and delightful at night in that part of the country."

I leaned past him again. "You see? It isn't hot everywhere in India."

The woman I spoke to didn't answer. She was sleeping, her glass held in her lap with both hands, eyes closed and head against the sofa.

Henry Hunter offered me a cigarette. "So you think the tea business is romantic?" He seemed pleased, as if he acquired some romantic aura from contact with it. "That's what Lady Blanche thinks, too."

"I certainly agree with her! It's thrilling to know of those exotic, faraway places your teas come from, and all the different things a man in your position must learn. You know"—I hesitated and then began to talk rapidly as the idea developed—"my publishers want another romantic novel from me, something that will sell to the movies. I've been racking my brain for a suitable background, the right kind of man for my hero. But since I met you—and I'm sure you understand that it takes something as apparently trivial as our acquaintanceship to spark the whole thing—I've been thinking all evening of what a thrilling novel could be written about the tea trade. We had a flat tire on the way over here, and while we sat waiting for the tire to be changed, I began to make mental notes about a possible story."

He moved around to face me. "You did? What kind of story, for instance?"

"Well"—I lowered my voice to confidential pitch—"if you take this man, for instance, who is manager of a tea importing firm . . ."

He finished his drink and set it down without looking at the table.

Smoke curled unnoticed from his cigarette in the ashtray. And I went on talking.

## CHAPTER SIX

I WAS SURPRISED the next morning when I wandered into the living room, yawning, to find Lily there, not yet dressed. I had taken for granted that she would already have gone to the clinic. When I mentioned this she said, "Li Tsui-Yi will be here to visit us soon." She didn't mention how the sick woman would get to our house. "Are you ready to eat?"

"In ten minutes." I started for the shower.

When I came out again I found breakfast served in the garden and Lily waiting. It was quiet there, and cool in the shadow of the mango tree. Lily looked herself again, her hair tied with a ribbon, sleeves of her thin kimono pinned back at the shoulders. We settled at the table, ready to talk.

I began at random, holding a hand over the lime I squeezed onto my papaya. "What about Lady Blanche Carleton? Last night she said that her husband had died suddenly. Do you suppose . . .?" I left the words in the air, faintly aghast at my own thought processes.

"You knew, Lily," I went on, "before I met you I would not have thought of a melodramatic thing like that."

"Like murder?" she said. "It depends on what climate you live in." She wasn't speaking geographically. "To most people, of course, it is melodrama. To others—" She ate a spoonful of melon and shrugged.

I flipped a lime seed toward the lily pond. Two mynas swooped for it and collided in midair. The victor grabbed the seed, spat it out, and reviled me with raucous squawks. Lily and I laughed, then I took up where I'd left off.

"Do you suppose the Waikiki Widow murdered her husband?"

Lily poured coffee. "She does not seem to be the type. Of course, there is not really a 'type.' What matters is provocation." She handed me a cup and asked, "What impression did you get of Lacy Blanche?"

I considered it. "Well . . . I agree with Alan Hart that she is fascinating. Most women are fairly easy to size up, but I can't figure this one. Taking her features apart, you find that she isn't beautiful, but there's something about her she seems to generate excitement."

I fumbled mentally for clarifying words and found none. "On the other hand," I added, "I think she's frivolous and vain, and very likely has been pampered all her life. She's obviously used to having plenty of money—"

"Why do you say that?"

"Oh, her clothes, the way she wears them. The kind of party she gave for us—"

"Henry Hunter paid the check last night."

"Oh."

"And the party was not really for your Hollywood crowd—they aren't important to her. It was a means of entertaining him. He is happy to pay for such entertainment."

"In order to associate with glamorous people?"

"Possibly."

"Tell me more about the lady. I won't challenge your source of information. I know you're always sure of your facts."

Lily smiled and said, "*Hoomalimali.*"

"It's not flattery. Go ahead."

"Blanche Carleton was born in Liverpool into what is considered in England a lower class family. She went out to Singapore as a nurse, and Sir Simon became her patient. He was twenty-two years her senior, in chronic poor health. She was known among the hospital staff, incidentally, as a woman who had a great deal of what the French politely term 'temperament'."

"But she decided to forgo what we Americans vulgarly call 'a good toss in the hay' in favor of a rich old husband."

Lily nodded. "Correct. However, when Sir Simon took her to England on a visit, she discovered that, like many of his class, he was land poor. Aside from his diplomatic pay, he hadn't a penny. So when he was ordered home, she must have known that they were on their way to a life very different from the one they knew in China. Incidentally, since by birth she is a commoner, she has no right to call herself Lady Blanche. Her correct title as a widow is Blanche, Lady Carleton."

"Who cares?"

"The British."

That didn't matter to me. "At this point," I said, "tell me something—did Sir Simon have life insurance?"

"Yes. It was payable to his sister, who lives on their estate in Sussex. She is fifty-six and breeds Sealyhams. Their house has eighteen rooms and one bath. There is no central heating."

"Did Lady Blanche know this?"

"Yes. He changed beneficiaries quite a long time ago, after he had to pay his wife's accumulated gambling debts. Their marriage seems to have reached a kind of climax then. She was also rumored to be having an affair with some American. I don't have any details of that."

"You have plenty, it seems to me. Is she one of those women who can't resist gambling?"

"She used to be. From the way she behaved last night, she seems not to have changed. That's why I arranged the party at Ing's place. I need to reach her in some way, and if she's like most British colonials, normal social contact with any other race is something she's incapable of."

"Isn't gambling illegal in Honolulu?"

"The Ings don't run a gambling house, they merely entertain their friends. No money changes hands under their roof—they play with chips. The day after you visit them a messenger calls and either pays what you have won or collects your losses. Blanche Carleton was much amused when this was explained to her. She will probably want to go there again. I hope so, for then she will discover that the only way she can return is with a 'friend.' "

"How did you find out so much about her?"

"From Betty Chang. Betty's father was a banker. He got his money out of China before the government collapsed. Betty didn't know Blanche Carleton—she was only thirteen then—but her elder sister played around with the international set. Blanche was part of it."

"And no doubt Sir Simon strongly disapproved. What did he die of?"

"He was a diabetic. He collapsed into a coma three weeks before they were scheduled to sail for England by way of the United States."

"It is easy to kill a diabetic," I said.

"Oh yes," Lily agreed. "For a nurse there are many easy ways to murder."

She pushed her coffee cup aside and shook a cigarette from the pack on the table. "Whether this woman killed her husband does not seem to pertain to our problem, except possibly to indicate the kind of person she is. It seems to me that we must concentrate on other angles."

"Such as—"

"Yao. He was her houseboy—that must be significant." She lit her cigarette and said through smoke, "If I had not come home to change clothes yesterday, if I had stayed and forced Yao to talk—" Her voice had sharpened and she stopped and resumed in a lower tone "That silly masquerade last night must pay off *somehow!*"

I asked, "What about Yao? There haven't been any police here to question us. Was there an autopsy? Does anyone know what happened?"

"Ethel called early this morning. Yao died from internal injuries as the result of being crushed by a car. Police have found the car, which was reported stolen at nine o'clock last night. The tire pattern matches the marks on Yao's shirt, and there were pink carnation petals in the right front spring. No fingerprints. It was a Ford sedan belonging to a naval officer who lives in Manoa, and the car was taken from his garage some time after four o'clock, when he and his wife went to a cocktail party with friends."

"Where was the car found?"

"Parked on Tenth Street in Kaimuki."

"That's on the way back from the Blow Hole. So the driver returns to Honolulu, parks the car on a quiet street, and calmly takes the bus into town. But a man doesn't lie down at command, like a dog, and permit a car to drive over him. Was there any other mark on Yao's body?"

"Bruises on his head. They could have been caused by striking the curbing, if he was hit crossing an intersection."

"The car was reported stolen at nine, and that news story was on the streets by six. Ten thousand people could have read it. But you say Yao didn't know anyone here. He wouldn't have gone out to meet a stranger. And it was a woman who called. Miss Ching heard music over the phone. Lily, I think it was Blanche Carleton."

"I am not so sure. Any waitress, clerk, or switchboard operator would have made such a call at the request of a tourist, for instance. And there is music all over this island. Blanche had opportunity to call from the Royal, but we know that she did not drive the car. And the nurse said Yao was speaking Chinese. There were insulting remarks made to Lady Blanche in several dialects last night and she did not show the slightest reaction. She may have seen the paper. In that case it seems more likely that she got in touch with someone else who made the call. Our problem is to discover who that person is."

I said, appalled at the possibility, "There may be some sort of gang—"

Lily looked quickly at me. "That is possible. I hope not."

"Tiger. Dragon." I puzzled. "They sound like symbols. Are they the kind of Chinese words which could mean several different things, depending on context?"

"No. I read the characters correctly." She looked thoughtful as she added, "Yao knew how the Lis' fortune was being smuggled here from China by way of British Hong Kong. He said that the smuggling was connected with tea. Blanche Carleton now associates with the manager of a tea importing firm—did you find out what that connection is?"

"Yes. Mr. Hunter told me last night." I repeated his story of the lady's thirst for a rare China tea, Henry Hunter's obtaining it for her, delivering it in person, and so on.

"So," Lily said, "last night was profitable, after all. Now we need to find out many other things. How this smuggling is being done, for instance—"

That was when I interrupted. "I don't know anything about tea shipments," I said. "But I'm sure that everything coming into this country has to go through some kind of customs. I'm equally sure that American inspectors are very smart. So, how can a fortune possibly be smuggled in a shipment of tea?"

Lily hesitated, then said carefully, "Yesterday, Li Tsui-Yi refused permission to tell you. But Harry and Ethel reassured her about our relationship, and when I called her this morning Yao's death made her realize that we need all the help we can get. It is a long and involved story, and she prefers to tell it herself. But I can give you a little of her history. I said yesterday that she is thirty-eight. That happens to be the same age, incidentally, as Blanche Carleton. When I knew Li Tsui-Yi in China she was a beautiful woman. You have seen what she looks like now."

I contrasted two thirty-eight-year-old women who had come here from the Orient, one with hollow eyes in a shrunken face crowned by lifeless hair, the other a delicate-skinned, scented blonde. I thought of Blanche dancing in satin slippers, and I remembered a sheeted frame hiding mutilated feet on an iron hospital bed.

I said, "What can Madame Li own that is worth half a million dollars and is still small enough to be smuggled out of China?"

"Jewels," Lily said. "The Li fortune was in the form of pearls. They are very rare because they came from—"

Shizu appeared on the balcony. "Doctor Chun called. He is bringing someone to see you."

Lily started from the chaise. "And we aren't dressed yet!" She hurried up the steps and I followed.

## CHAPTER SEVEN

MADAME LI CAME into our house in a wheelchair of the light collapsible type, pushed by Doctor Harry Chun. Lily stepped forward and bowed low, murmuring a greeting. While our guest responded I had a chance to smooth amazement from my face.

Here was no haggard wreck of a woman painful to look upon. Still frail to transparency, still hollow-eyed, yes—but with a difference. She wore white, the color of mourning, but her dress was of silk unobtainable now, its brocade design richer than finest embroidery. Her hair had been shampooed and carefully arranged and there was faint color on her lips. Under penciled brows her eyes were large and black. They blazed with intelligence.

While I welcomed her I said a small prayer to the gods. If ever I must lose what I hold dear, take success, my bank account, my looks—but leave with me the spark of a brave spirit.

She glanced around our living room with interest; and on impulse

I said, "Madame Li, would you like to see our house?" If I had been Chinese I would have used polite words like humble and unworthy—but I spoke in English.

She said in a clear, flutelike voice, "Yes, I should like to see it. I am most curious."

I took her on a brief tour through bedrooms and kitchen and finished with the view from our balcony. When I turned the chair around Harry had gone and Shizu was bringing in a tray. We formed a threesome around the *k'ang* where Lily was seated. She poured tea into thin cups, then offered our guest a compartmented dish containing watermelon seeds, preserved walnuts, sweetened lotus, and died ginger. She and Madame Li, I noticed, raised their cups with both hands.

I have learned from Lily that if one finds it necessary to maintain poise for an indefinite time, it is easier to do so with a straight spine. I chose a high-backed chair, pushed my backbone against it, took a sip of tea, and waited. When Madame Li set down her cup I knew that talk was about to begin.

The Chinese woman addressed me. "Hsui-Ming has told me about your friendship. She informs me that you have shared dangers, that you helped her in a time of trouble, and that she once saved your life and is therefore responsible for you. How do you like being the foster daughter of a Chinese family?

I answered, "I have not adequate vocabulary to tell you all that I feel I will say only that I consider myself privileged."

She smiled. "Spoken almost like a Chinese. This is the first time that a fair-haired person has sat at the Wu family table. At least you do not have pale eyes."

I didn't know what she meant by that, except that my eyes are dark brown instead of the blue which usually goes with fair hair. I glanced at Lily and saw that she was frowning slightly as if trying to remember something. When Madame Li turned to her she dismissed the effort and became attentive.

"What have you told Miss Cameron?"

"I was waiting for you to arrive."

Madame Li folded her hands into her lap and looked at the silk coverlet wrapped around her legs and feet. "I suppose," she said to me, "that you know the story of Tz'u Hsi?"

"She was the Empress Dowager, called Old Buddha. The Manchu dynasty ended with her death in 1908. Wasn't she buried with several million dollars worth of treasure in a supposedly impregnable tomb?"

"Which was violated about twenty years later. Some of the jewels and art objects from the tomb still appear from time to time in the hands of collectors all over the world."

She looked at Lily. "Does she know of my family?"

"No."

"My father," Madame Li said, "was a court official in the Forbidden City. He hired managers for his lands and various holdings, which included a fishing fleet. His tribute to the Empress was in the form of pearls, so precious that they were among the choicest gems which adorned her corpse."

My face must have shown incredulity. Madame Li's fingers went to her collar and she pulled out a thin chain. Swinging from the end of it was a pearl which glowed even against the rich silk of her dress. I leaned toward it involuntarily.

The Chinese woman said, "Many people covet such beauty. There were a hundred of these." She hid the pearl again and said to Lily, "I should like a cigarette, please."

She took a few puffs and discarded it. When she began again her voice had grown weaker. "Now, I will speak of my husband. He was a man who greatly loved China. He believed that our country's future lies in the hands of her youth—her educated youth—and he dedicated his life to them as guardians of China's destiny. After the communists came into power he chose to remain and continue his work in agriculture because he said the land would never change, it would belong to the people no matter which powers developed it. But he began then to help students leave the country in order to study elsewhere. After they were educated, he said, they would choose what government they wanted, but they must have a complete education in order to be able to judge.

"We sent many students from Hangchow, where we lived. Their parents gave what money they could, friends contributed. Fishermen who formerly worked for my father smuggled them to Hong Kong."

I asked, "Is that how you escaped?"

"Yes. After my husband's death I consented to leave. Since I could not walk, I was carried to the coast. I lay on the deck of a sampan, under a pile of nets, for two days. I brought with me only a few pieces of gold jewelry—and one pearl."

"The pearls—"

"Yes. My mind wanders—I am growing tired. My husband had the pearls which had been my father's tribute to Tz'u Hsi. They were returned to us through channels which I cannot divulge. Li kept them. He said I would be safer if I knew nothing. We were planning then to leave. Since the authorities were suspicious, he entrusted the pearls to a friend who would return them to us when we reached Hong Kong. We intended to sell them and use the money—"

The door chime sounded. Madame Li leaned back and closed her eyes. Lily admitted Harry Chun and he went to the invalid and picked up her wrist. She whispered, "Enough?"

"More than enough," he told her. "You must say good-by now."

At the door she said, sitting erect again, "Yao will be buried this afternoon. Do not attend."

Lily said, "No. Nor will anyone go to the airport with you."

"It is not necessary. Mildred Ching will take good care of me. Good-by, Miss Cameron, and thank you for showing me your house. I shall tell the Wus all about it."

"Good-by." I hesitated, then added, "*Aloha nui loa.*"

Her eyes thanked me. Harry wheeled her out the door. The sound of the car faded down the hill.

Lily and I sat down and lit cigarettes, and I said, "Go on with the story. Before the Lis could leave Hangchow, apparently, their house was broken into and both were questioned under torture. Because of the pearls?"

"Yes."

"Who did it?"

Lily shrugged. "What happened does not sound like police methods. There were only two men. Tsui-Yi did not know who they were, for they wore masks. She knew they were educated men since they spoke fluent Mandarin. She fainted, and when she recovered consciousness she had been put in another room and heard her husband being tortured by means of—"

"No!" I cried. "I don't want to hear that part of it. What about the Lis' plan for using money from the sale of the pearls?"

Lily poured a cup of tea and sipped it. She said, "There are several thousand young Chinese nationals in the United States today, enrolled in various universities. They have inadequate means of support. Stranded in Hong Kong are former educators and professional men—sociologists, engineers, experts on political science. I had to obtain drugs and other necessities for the Chinese doctor who attended Madame Li. He had no equipment of any kind."

"Why not?"

"He sold everything to get food. He had become a street beggar. The suicide rate in Hong Kong now almost equals the number of deaths from starvation."

She began to unscrew jade buttons from her ears. "Yao will be buried this afternoon. Li Tsui-Yi leaves for New York in a few hours. You and I have made one step toward solution of this problem. One small step."

"Lily," I said, "let me quote something Chinese: 'The longest journey begins with a single step.' Isn't that right?"

"More or less. What are you looking so smug about?"

"I'll tell you." I was feeling pretty good at that moment. "You asked about the Waikiki Widow and Henry Hunter, and I repeated what he told me last night at the hotel. I didn't repeat the conversation we had at the Ings' place later."

She laid the earrings on the chow bench and waited.

"—and so," I concluded, "he suggested that the best way to do research about tea might be to observe how the business is operated. When I said I'd had secretarial experience he was quite pleased. We arranged that I am to start work in the office of Paradise Teas at eight tomorrow morning."

## CHAPTER EIGHT

HENRY HUNTER'S OFFICE was in an older section of Honolulu, on Maunakea Street. The building was a two-storied wooden rectangle, narrow and drab. A sign swung over the sidewalk: "HALE-

KOKUA. Hollis Knight." Below that, in smaller letters, was "Paradise Teas, Ltd."

Businesses here bore no resemblance to flossy tourist shops at Waikiki. An old Chinese sat in the doorway of his tiny jewelry store smoking a pipe, the shop next to his displayed cheap underwear, brush and comb sets on faded rayon satin, stacks of grass sandals and straw hats. Other windows bore undecipherable Oriental characters and layers of grime.

I opened the door and found myself, surprisingly, in a reception room which was the color of driftwood, curtained with matchstick bamboo. Begonias bloomed in window stands. There were rattan chairs cushioned in green pebble cloth. Since it was thirty minutes past office opening time, someone should have been at the desk, but it was not occupied and the typewriter beside it was covered.

I looked around the room, my first pleasant impression modified by sight of unemptied ashtrays and dust on the furniture. There were two closed doors—one behind the desk and the other at the right side of the room—and as I waited facing them I made circles in the dust of the desk with a forefinger. The rear door opened suddenly and a blonde teetered in, carrying a soiled white purse and a paperback sex novel. She wore too much lipstick. She laid purse and book down and rolled the chair back without bothering to say good morning. After she was seated she looked at me and said, "You wanna see somebody?"

"Why yes, I—"

She scowled at marks I had made on the desk and covered them with her purse. She said, with the sneer of one-who-has for one-who-needs, "I can give you a blank to fill out but there's no use. Nothing available."

I said, trying to maintain civility, "I'd like to see Mr. Hunter."

"Hunter?" She took a dirty rag from a drawer and wiped the desk. "That won't do any good."

"Will you tell him I'm here, please? Miss Cameron."

She snatched the cover from her typewriter and rammed it into a drawer. "I said there's nothing open."

For a moment I began to relive experiences when, already going through the ordeal of having to petition for a chance to earn a living, I had been subjected to similar humiliations. I could feel my face growing hot.

I said curtly, "Mr. Hunter expects me."

"Oh." She gave me a quick, curious glance. "He's not here yet. Come back later."

I stepped close to her. "Look, you insolent cretin. I am a personal friend of Henry Hunter's and he asked me to come to his office this morning. If he isn't available, I want to see someone in authority here. And damned quick!"

Her eyes bugged. She reached for the intercom, then swiveled her chair, and I turned to see what she was looking at. The door on the right had opened and Jean Hunter stood there. I didn't know how much she had overheard. She said in a frigid voice, "My uncle isn't in yet. Can I help you?"

Her face looked as pale as it had been before. Her gray eyes, fringed with thick straight lashes, were guarded. I itched to put lipstick on that colorless mouth, to give the girl a cheerful accent somewhere. She glanced at the staring receptionist and said, "Come in."

I needed time to figure how to approach her. There was a gray steel desk near the window and I took the chair in front of it, forcing her to come around and face me. She didn't sit down.

I began, "Perhaps you remember meeting me with other guests of Lady Blanche Carleton . . ."

The girl stiffened and the guarded look changed to hostility. Mention of that name was unfortunate.

I said quickly, "I am a writer, the author of the book which is being filmed here in Hawaii now. I mentioned to Mr. Hunter that I'm interested in the tea business, and he was kind enough to invite me here."

"The tea business," she said, "seems to interest all kinds of people lately."

Best to ignore that. "I might explain further that I am not a tourist. I was born here." I tried a smile and offered, "My interest in tea is practical, since I'm doing research for a novel. Your uncle offered me the opportunity to observe how this business operates."

She sat down behind the desk. "I don't know—Uncle Henry

hasn't said anything—he didn't come in yesterday—he wasn't feeling well. And this morning he is supposed to meet—an old family friend is arriving from China."

"China?"

At this point Henry Hunter came into the office. His shoulders drooped, and his fresh white suit accentuated the stubble on his face and his tired, bloodshot eyes. "Well, Jeanie," he said heartily, "the old boy fooled you this time. You probably thought I'd never make it but here I—" He stopped when he saw me.

I rose and said, "Good morning, Mr. Hunter. I've come to take advantage of your kindness."

He looked puzzled, then smiled as he remembered. "Miss Cameron. Janice, isn't it? Of course. Of course."

He hung up his hat and went to his desk. Jean Hunter moved to the smaller desk in the corner and sat in the typist's chair behind it. He said to her, "Miss Cameron wants to learn the tea business, Jeanie—she's writing a story about us."

"So she told me. But, Uncle Henry, aren't you supposed to be—"

"Meeting the President boat? Yes. But I stopped off here to shave. Called the harbormaster before I left the house and he said it'll be an hour yet before they get through customs."

He explained to me, "A very old friend of my wife's is arriving today from Canton."

"I didn't know anybody could leave China now."

"Matt's a missionary, been in China for years. They're letting the missionaries out—glad to get rid of them, no doubt."

He dismissed that subject, saying, "We'll try to get you settled right away. Jean's been working as my secretary, and I thought—"

He turned to his niece. "She can use your desk for a while. That will give you a chance, Jeanie, to get back to your own work."

I wondered what that work was. He had said that since his wife died Jean had been trying to take over. He didn't want her in his office. I glanced at the girl and saw by the tightening of her mouth that she was determined to stay.

She said, ignoring me, "This job requires training."

"I'm a stenographer," I told her. As she continued to look stubborn I added, "Let me try to estimate what the work involves. Correspondence, payroll, invoices and bills of lading, orders, statements to customers—"

"Ha!" Henry Hunter exclaimed. "I'll bet you can even remember the names of our island towns."

"Kahului," I began. "Lahaina. Hilo. Nawiliwili, Kona, Kaunakakai, Laupahoehoe"—I stopped for breath, then added—"I can even spell them."

He slapped his hand on the desk. "That's more than Jean here can do. You're hired! When can you start?"

He had forgotten our arrangement. I said, "Today, if you wish." I nodded toward the smaller desk. "Is this your secretary's corner?"

"Right. You can take possession right now. Suppose you use my desk this morning, Jean, while you show this girl the ropes. You can probably go home after lunch."

Jean Hunter's eyes glittered. "I can't. I have to stay and help you." She sent him a significant look. "There's a shipment coming in on the President boat."

There was immediate tension in the room. The smile left his face, he drummed the desk, snatched a cigarette package, found it empty, and tossed it irritably to the floor.

I said, "Would you like one of mine?" and he took it gratefully and got very busy with matches. I held the pack toward Jean Hunter and she started to accept and then dropped her hand. "No, thanks." The next, to her uncle, was accusatory. "And *you* shouldn't, either."

He crushed out the cigarette, while I looked at the floor and decided that she really was an insufferable little prig. Henry was studying the ashtray. He started when she said, "The shipment, Uncle Henry."

"Oh yes. Yes, of course, the Darjeeling."

"No." She looked fixedly at him.

"No? That hasn't come yet?"

He evaded her eyes, he shuffled through the incoming correspondence box, found what he sought, and read hastily. The paper shook in his hands.

The girl said, "This is the tea you ordered for Mr. Oka."

He dropped the papers. "The Hachiogi. Oh yes, yes. Don't worry, Jeanie. I'll be back. After I meet Matt Webster."

They exchanged looks, his conveying a sort of shamed defiance, hers a question and reproach.

I was embarrassed. To avoid watching them I rose and went to look at a framed portrait on the wall of an old gentleman in rich robes, mandarin's button on his hat, beads in his long fingers, a look of profound sadness in the deep-set eyes of his thin, ascetic face.

Henry Hunter said, "That's Chinnery's portrait of Houqua. If the tea business had a patron saint, old Houqua would be it. In twenty-five years of dealing with American tea merchants he never used a contract or written promise—and he never broke his word. His kind doesn't exist any more."

The girl came over to stand before the portrait. She said in a musing voice, "An El Greco in Chinese robes. I wish I could have painted him."

I asked, with the first friendly feeling I'd been able to generate, "Are you an artist?"

"Yes."

Her uncle spoke from behind a door which concealed a lavatory. "Jean's responsible for the redecorating that's been going on around here. But that's not her line. She's a very good designer. She's been neglecting her work to help me."

He turned a faucet and opened the medicine cabinet. "Why don't you take Miss Cameron around, honey, while I shave? I don't want to meet Matt with this beard."

She looked at me. "Would you like to see the place now?"

I followed her into a large room with rows of tables where a dozen girls were seated, measuring tea into packages which passed to the end of the table to be sealed. Jean Hunter explained in a low voice, while workers—neatly blue-uniformed girls of a dozen mixed bloods, mostly Oriental, Portuguese, and Filipino—looked up curiously and then smiled with the natural friendliness of islanders. We went into another room where a big metal tumbler stood, and Jean said that it was a blender.

"Almost all teas are blended—that is, leaves of different types and quality are put into the tumbler in certain proportions and mixed."

"Like mixing a cake."

"Yes. Except, of course, tea must be dry. Moisture would be disastrous."

"How are blends made up? By a sort of prescription?"

"The tea-taster decides. Every firm has its individual blends. That's how tea reputations are made."

"Tea-taster?"

"Each company has one, and some large firms have several. When a tea crop is offered for sale, a few ounces are sent by air to prospective buyers, whose tasters sample the teas and give their opinion to the owner. He then—"

"Excuse me," I said "You mentioned the owner. Who owns this firm? I understand your uncle is the manager."

"The owner lives in New York, where we have a sales office. He retired recently, and his son took over the business. It doesn't amount to much there—most of our teas are marketed locally."

"Then the owner doesn't decide which teas are to be purchased?"

"Not this one. Mr. Brittain used to come here twice a year to check over the business, but Uncle Henry makes most of the decisions. He has worked for the Brittains for many years."

"I see. So after the taster reports on these crops which are offered for sale . . . ?"

"The manager instructs the grower's representative in the place the tea comes from. Formosa, Japan, India—"

"China?"

"That used to be one of the most important sources of supply. No tea comes from China now."

"Sorry for the interruption."

"So the tea buyer bids on the crop at auction, up to the figure authorized by the importer. Then, when the tea is shipped, another sample is sent—a 'forward mail sample' it is called—by air. When the shipment arrives it is tested first by the local tea examiner to make sure that a certain quality is maintained. When it reaches our warehouse it goes through a final test. Tea from the shipment must agree in quality with the two previous samples."

"I had no idea it was so complicated."

"It is simple, really."

I asked, "And who does the tea-tasting here?"

"My uncle," she said, and walked ahead of me. "I'll show you the warehouse now."

"Just a minute." I glanced through an open door into a small room which contained a round table with a Lazy Susan top. A tea kettle stood on an electric plate in a corner, under shelves which held many little square boxes. "Is this the tasting room?"

She halted, but did not come back. "Yes." Since she was waiting for me I followed, reluctantly. We reached the warehouse at the rear of the building, where chests of tea were ranged on shelves under various labels. Jean Hunter rattled off names of different varieties and I walked the length of the big room with her, while I began to feel certain of a focal point for the tension I had felt since I arrived. It concerned tea shipments. I would have to find out more about these shipments. In the meantime it would be important to learn the names of different kinds of tea. Was there one called Dragon Tea? Or Tiger Tea? And if so, where had it come from? Or had it arrived?

A door near us opened, and light streamed into the dim warehouse. Hollis Knight stood outside on a wooden loading platform. Behind him I saw stairs angling upward. He didn't see me; he was looking at the girl.

"Can you come up for a minute, Jean? We're working on your layout, and I want to check a few things."

"After a while, Hollis. I'm busy now."

The door closed and the warehouse was dim again. I looked at her and she said, "Those stairs lead to *Halekokua*, Mr. Knight's place of business. He owns the building. We rent this floor from him."

"*Halekokua*," I repeated. "And is it really a house of cooperation?"

She sent me a quick glance. "I will take you up there later. You can see for yourself."

"And that girl in the reception room," I said as we started back, "does she work for Mr. Knight?"

"Yes. Hollis is an importer. Her job is to receive buyers. She also admits callers to Paradise Teas. That reminds me—she has an extra key to the office. I'll get it for you now."

After she gave me the key I waited while she removed a few personal things from the secretary's desk. Jean's uncle had gone. The bottom drawer of his desk was pulled out, and lying with its neck on the edge of the drawer was a bottle labeled "Martell." If Henry Hunter had reached a point where he needed brandy pickups in the morning, no wonder his hands shook. Then my eyes focused on a compartment toward the rear of the drawer where a folder lay. I bent to pick up the crumpled cigarette package. As my fingers closed over the paper I looked into the drawer. From that angle I could read the label of the folder. It said: "T.B. Confidential."

Jean Hunter was watching me. She rose swiftly and came to the desk to close the drawer. I tossed the cigarette package into the wastebasket and dusted my hands. Neither of us made any comment. She went back to the corner, opened a filing cabinet behind the secretary's chair, and took out another folder, which she spread an the desk.

"Now," she said crisply, "these are customers on Kauai, listed alphabetically. The ones marked X buy the cheaper variety of Orange Pekoe . . ." She pronounced it to rhyme with peck instead of peek.

We worked until Henry Hunter returned, bringing with him the friend whom he had gone to meet. He was a man of medium height, wearing white drill which hung loosely on a very thin frame. His hair and eyebrows were snowy white and he had pale amber eyes set in a tanned, cadaverous face. He wore a pink carnation lei.

Henry said, "This is our old friend, Matthew Webster. He's just arrived from Canton."

Mr. Webster acknowledged introductions in a deep voice, adding, "I'm not so ancient as I look, you know. Just recovering from a bout with dysentery. It weakens one." He looked around the office. "So this is where you preside, Henry. It doesn't look the way you described it in your letters."

"Jean has just redecorated it for me."

Henry went to his desk. He removed the bottle and poured brandy into a paper cup. When the missionary shook his head, smiling, Henry drank it himself.

Jean Hunter said, eyed fixed on the bottle, "Are you going to take Mr. Webster home now? Or do you think he could wait while we open the tea? There are only three chests."

Henry looked at Matthew Webster. "Would you mind waiting while I get this job done? It won't take half an hour."

"Certainly. I'll sit and admire this pleasant office."

Henry followed his niece out, and since they had not invited me,

I had to remain there and entertain the visitor.

I began, "You have a very nice tan, Mr. Webster."

"I have, haven't I?" He seemed pleased. "There was little to do on board ship except lie in the sun. And I was glad, of course, to get the rest. Life has been pretty hectic in the past months."

"How did you manage to get out of China? Over here we have the impression that no one can cross the border."

"For missionary workers it is not impossible. One goes through interminable red tape, of course. For example, I had to advertise in the local paper for seven days that I planned to leave the country, so that creditors could collect what was due them. Then I had to take my personal servant to the police, where he was questioned about the treatment I gave my domestic staff. When he gave me a good character I was permitted to discharge the servants after paying them three months' salary."

"Good heavens! They're certainly careful, aren't they?"

"That's not all. After being vouched for by my servants, I had to obtain a letter signed with the chop of a local Chinese merchant who guaranteed payment of any uncollected debts. Then I was given an exit permit, routed through Canton."

There was an awkward little silence while I wished I knew what Jean and her uncle were doing. I forced myself to be polite again and remarked that I hadn't the vaguest idea what a missionary did when he wasn't working in a foreign field.

He said, "Some of us go back to theological seminary, others take a leave of absence. In my case there is little choice. I'm returning because of ill health. Henry has persuaded me to visit him for a while before I sail. I haven't been out of China for eighteen years, and once I'm back in Missouri . . ." He finished with a tired smile.

"Did you learn Chinese?"

"Oh yes. Not thoroughly, of course. That takes a lifetime. But I speak it well enough. My station was in Ningpo. I heard from a friend at the Church Guest House in Hong Kong that the mission was burned after I left."

Silence again.

Henry and Jean had not returned. I said, hoping for a chance to follow them, "Would you like to see how the business is conducted, Mr. Webster? That is, of course, if walking does not tire you too much . . ."

He rose slowly, gripping the arms of the chair. "I'd enjoy that. But I'll leave this here, if you don't mind. It's uncommonly warm." He laid the pink flowers on Henry's desk by the brandy bottle.

When we reached the tasting room I tried the knob. The door was locked. Jean Hunter opened it and said, "I'm sorry, but my uncle won't admit anyone while he's tasting." She shut the door again.

At that moment Hollis Knight appeared, looking for Jean. I told him where she was, then introduced him to Mr. Webster. When he heard that the missionary had just arrived from Hong Kong, he said, "How are things over there? I'm due for a trip pretty soon. Haven't made one for four months now."

"Very crowded. And of course, the cost of living is fantastically high."

They started talking and after hanging around for a minute I left them with the excuse that I had better go back to work.

I went directly to Henry Hunter's desk and opened the bottom drawer, then almost jumped out of my skin as the telephone rang. I kicked the drawer shut as I answered it.

The voice was familiar. "Mr. Hunter, please."

"He can't come to the phone just now," I said. "May I take a message?"

"He cannot come to the telephone?" She was haughty. "Tell him that Lady Blanche Carleton is on the wire."

"I'm sorry, Lady Blanche," I said. "Mr. Hunter is in the tasting room. This is Janice Cameron speaking. I'll ask him to call you as soon as he comes out. He knows your number, of course."

"Certainly he— Oh no, this is a new one. That is what I wanted to tell him. Janice Cameron—oh, of course! You came to my little party with Alan Hart. And what, my dear, are you doing in Henry's office?"

"Learning all about the tea business," I told her, my tone as playful as hers. "I'm to be Mr. Hunter's secretary for a little while."

"How clever of you! By the way, Miss Cameron, I am glad of this chance to invite you for supper this evening. It is really a sort of house-warming, since I have just moved into my new house. Can you come?"

"I'll be delighted. It is very kind of you to ask me."

"Not at all. And do bring that adorable little friend of yours."

"You mean Lily Wu?"

"Yes. I'd like to know her better. I found her utterly fascinating."

"I'll bring her if she's free."

"Please do. Sevenish? And now, will you be a good secretary and write down my new number for Henry?"

I wrote it on a scratch pad. As I wrote, my arm brushed the carnation lei which the missionary had discarded. The warm still air was heavy with its perfume. Sensual stimulus is a quicker avenue to memory, perhaps, than any other. The sound of Blanche Carleton's voice and the strong carnation fragrance brought in a rush the image I had been successful up to now in suppressing.

Yao. Yao, incredulous at his good fortune at having reached America. Yao, going to the telephone to hear, magically, the voice of the woman who formerly employed him, welcoming him here, perhaps—was that how it had been done?—or possibly saying that she knew of a fine job, that a friend of hers would bring him to see her.

The friend. Faceless, voiceless to me, but whose presence seemed momentarily to invade the room. The friend who called softly to Yao, opened the door of the car and invited, speaking the tongue which Yao spoke, who closed the door of the car and drove off into the soft warm night. To stop again—where? In an alley, perhaps, where there was darkness and silence. The sudden cruel blow. The drive continued, the stop on a deserted stretch of highway, to lay Yao's breathing body on the ground, put the car into, low gear . . . the bump forward . . . the horrible bump of the tires back again . . .

The door opened. I jerked and stared, hand over my mouth to stifle an outcry, at people entering the room. Jean Hunter, her uncle, and Hollis Knight, behind them the missionary. Henry Hunter seemed surprised to see me in his chair, and his niece was frowning.

I said in an unnatural voice. "Excuse me for using your desk, Mr. Hunter. I just took a telephone call from Lady Blanche Carleton."

I indicated the scratch-pad and attempted a smile which felt on my stiff lips like a grimace.

Henry said, "Don't you feel well?"

"It's the heat, the smell of the flowers. I'm perfectly fine, really." I went to the lavatory and splashed cold water on my face, glad of an excuse to regain my composure.

Lily had been right, as usual, and I determined never to permit myself such betraying emotions again. At that moment I loathed all of them.

## CHAPTER NINE

"NOW YOU'VE HEARD the story of my delightful day," I said to Lily. We were driving toward Blanche Carleton's house at Waikiki. "Suppose you tell me what you've been doing."

Lily touched the fine black fringe across her brow. "I have been busy. First, with the hairdresser."

"You actually had it cut?"

"Yes, and I hate it. But we are going to see as much of Lady Blanche as we can manage, and I must continue to look stupid."

"You couldn't look stupid."

"Frivolous, then, vapid—whatever you wish. Let's not talk about it. I also went shopping. My wardrobe didn't match this coiffure."

"I thought that demure little item you're wearing was new." It was purple taffeta with sequins and she wore gold kid sandals with two-inch platforms which made her feet look as if they had been bound.

"What else did you do today?"

"I wrote to my parents and to Madame Li. I called on a dozen people, in widely separated parts of Honolulu. This supper sounds interesting, but I hope there will not be too many guests."

"There may be a mob. I wonder how many of them we'll know. Here's the street."

We found the number on the opened gate of a high bamboo fence which enclosed the property. We turned in and parked beside someone's Buick, then walked toward the house.

"Isn't this the Fenwick place?" Lily asked, and I agreed that it was. I had seen pictures of it in the Sunday *Advertiser.* Cy Fenwick had built it for his ex-actress wife. She had signed a television contract, they had divorced, and the house had been empty since. Rumor said the rent was too high.

Apparently not too high for Lady Blanche. She greeted us with outstretched hands, saying, "How sweet of you to come and see my new home! It's fantastically vulgar, but I'm so delighted, after living like a cave dweller for ages, that I want to show it to everybody. Where do you wish to start—inside or out?"

"Anywhere at all," Lily said rudely, "so long as it leads to a bar. I've been rushing like mad all day and I'm so dehydrated it's pitiful."

"Come with me, my dear," our hostess said, and I followed them, wondering if my fastidious little friend enjoyed being vulgar for a change. I decided not. Centuries of social experience are inbred in Lily; and she is thoroughly Chinese in her preference for agreeable manners as being merely common sense.

I trailed along and listened while Lily prattled—in a voice half an octave higher than normal—admiration of the vast living room with sliding glass walls open to the evening, while she exclaimed that the free-form swimming pool with a lighted fountain at one end looked awfully cute, the marble-paved lanai was too sweet but thank God, here was the bar. To me the place was nightmarish, one of those modern houses which are all hard shiny surfaces, which contain every imaginable mechanical convenience and can never induce relaxation with out the aid of sedatives. Interior paneling, floors and fixtures had cost a fortune, but the decor—perhaps it is enough to say that the barroom furniture was upholstered in zebra skin.

When drinks were in our hands Blanche said, "Now you must see the bedrooms. They're too amusing for—" She broke off and called, "Hollis! Be a good chap, won't you, and take these girls around? I hear another car arriving."

Hollis Knight had been loitering near the door. He hurried in, saying, "Sure, Blanche. Be glad to. But—I don't know many of the people here."

"Show the rest of the house first, and be sure not to forget the aquarium. I'll do introductions when you're finished. Now, if you'll excuse me . . ." She went toward the driveway in a flutter of chiffon.

Hollis enjoyed this assignment. He took us through a couple of guest rooms and then to an extra-fancy room with an oversized bed, where he pulled a velvet spread down to show pastel satin sheets, saying, "Just have a look, if you want to see something gorgeous."

Next we were asked to admire an aquarium which stood against one wall on which was painted a submarine landscape. Hollis Knight turned a switch and lights glowed so that angelfish cast moving shadows on the underwater scene behind them. There was even a miniature diver poised on the bottom of the tank, air bubbles rising realistically from a tube attached to his helmet.

"Imagine the effect when the rest of the room is dark!" he said, and I answered that it certainly must be terrific, while I privately thought he sounded like a real estate agent.

When we returned to the lanai we found that Henry Hunter had brought Matthew Webster, who was sitting quietly in a chair while Henry talked with Blanche. More people arrived and were introduced: naval officers in uniform, tourists who were thrilled to enter "a real island home," some technicians from the Hollywood gang, and a few couples from Honolulu's fast set who are so bored with local diversions that they welcome every new face. The only friend we recognized was Gogo Leung; he saw us and headed in our direction, beaming. When he had captured Lily I went over to the missionary's chair.

"Hello, Mr. Webster—no, don't get up, please—I'll sit here. I hope you're feeling rested by now."

"Yes, thank you. I had a nap this afternoon. But I must confess that I feel slightly bewildered. This is quite different from anything in my previous experience. So much luxury—"

"To be perfectly honest with you, as I can't be with our hostess, I think it's horrible."

"You mean modern design? Are there many such houses now?"

He hadn't seen his country for eighteen years. I said, "There are plenty of modern houses, and some of them are wonderful, not like this. But I'm very rude to say so, when Lady Blanche is giving us such a nice party. Did you by any chance know her in China?"

"No. Henry says she was in Shanghai. My station was quite a distance away. I had never met the lady."

"I don't know her well," I said. "We've met only once before. Can I bring you something to drink, ginger ale, fruit juice?"

"I don't want a thing, thank you. And if I did, I'm quite capable of waiting on myself. I'm not completely an invalid. Am I, Henry?"

The last was addressed to Henry Hunter, who turned at the sound of his name. "An invalid? Of course you're not. Lady Blanche is very thrilled to hear that you've just come from China. She wants to talk with you." In spite of his effort to be courteous, his voice had sharpened. He seemed to resent Blanche's interest in the missionary.

She clung to Henry's arm as she said, "Indeed I do want to talk with you, Mr. Webster. Supper is being served now. I hope you can answer some of my questions while we eat. Did you spend much time in Hong Kong?"

"I'm afraid, Lady Blanche, that we won't find many mutual acquaintances . . ." he began, and I faded out to join Lily and Gogo. Hollis Knight followed me and when we left the buffet with our plates he took the fourth chair at our table on the lawn. We made the kind of small talk which is boring to exhaustion, in the course of which Hollis told us again, with a proprietorial tone, what a gorgeous place this was and that Lady Blanche was paying six hundred a month for it.

Finally he asked Gogo, "Doesn't your father own a lot of property in Macao?"

Gogo's face became very bland. "Somewhere around there. Do you know the Orient?"

"Sure. I make a buying trip four times a year. I'm an importer."

This was our cue to ask what he imported, but no one asked. He tried another question, this time of me. "I hear you're starting to work for Henry, you're going to write a story about tea."

"That's right."

"How long does it take to write a book like that?"

"It's difficult to say. A year, possibly. Maybe longer."

"How much will you get for it?"

"I haven't the vaguest idea. It might not even sell."

He looked incredulous, then his expression said that I must be a fool for spending a year of effort on such a hazardous project.

He tried Lily. "You've got some nice stones there, Miss Wu. Jewelry's something I know quite a bit about. They must have set somebody back plenty."

"These?" Lily glanced at her arm. She was wearing a new collection tonight, borrowed from Gogo's sister. Lily gave Hollis the vague smile which is the subtlest of insults and said, "Gogo. Please bring coffee."

Gogo took her plate while Hollis Knight carried mine back to the buffet. As soon as the men had gone, Lily said, "Blanche Carleton wants to go back to Ing's tonight. We're taking a party up there at eleven o'clock. You have the office key?"

"Yes. And a flashlight."

"You are sure the battery is good?"

"Of course. But I don't look forward to going into that building. Don't you think we might be rushing things a little?" I was trying to get out of my assignment and we both knew it.

Lily said apologetically, "I'm sorry you have to do this alone. But I don't think we are rushing anything. You tell me that Jean Hunter is hostile. Her uncle may protest that she interferes too much, but I believe that she will find some pretext for getting rid of you soon and that he will accept it. We would be foolish to disregard this opportunity. Here they come with our coffee."

"All right," I said under my breath. "I'll leave pretty soon."

At ten-thirty I went to the lanai where Blanche and Henry were dancing. They stopped at my approach.

"I have to be at my job early tomorrow," I said. "My boss is pretty strict." I winked at Henry Hunter and went on with conventional thank yous. As I spoke I noticed Matthew Webster in a chair behind a big tree fern. His eyes were closed.

Henry looked at his guest, then asked, "Would you mind taking Matt with you? He seems pretty tired, and I don't like to send him home in a taxi." The possibility of leaving Blanche Carleton's side never seemed to occur to him.

"Of course I don't mind. I'll be glad to take him." I wasn't the least bit glad, of course, but there was no way out of it. The Hunter house was directly on the way to my own.

We roused the missionary, who blinked and said apologetically that yes, he thought he'd better go to bed. We said very little on our way to Manoa. I didn't feel like talking and he seemed half asleep. As soon as he entered the house I started downtown in a hurry. I parked the car two blocks from Hollis Knight's building and walked along the deserted street with heels tapping and my long skirt swishing at every step.

The narrow structure loomed tall in the night and cast a long black shadow on the passage which led back to the loading platform. I fumbled with the key, inserted it upside down, jerked it out and tried again, and the door creaked open. I closed it behind me and leaned against the wood trying to listen for sounds which could not be heard above the thumping in my chest. I dared not use the flash. I inched across the reception room and bumped into the wall, groped for and found the knob of the door to Henry's office. Light from a street lamp seeped through the blinds and streaked the floor. My vision was better by then and I found the steel filing cabinet behind the secretary's desk and opened the first drawer, using the pencil flash from my purse to read labels on the manila folders.

Names of customers: Sugimoto, Choy, Jones, Perrera, Kikute, Nakamura, Won, Kaai, on the island of Maui; similar names on other islands, and with each a sheaf of invoice copies, bills of lading, carbons of correspondence regarding shipments and prices of teas. I scanned lists of varieties and found no tea named Dragon or Tiger. It would take hours, days perhaps, to go through this file.

I went to Henry Hunter's desk and opened the bottom drawer. The brandy bottle was almost empty now. I pulled the drawer out farther. The folder marked "T.B. Confidential" was still there and I lifted it.

What was that? Someone opening a door? A creak. Someone stepping on a loose floorboard? Or just the building settling in the night? I heard it again. I thrust the folder back and pushed the drawer shut. Cautious steps now, coming nearer, through the warehouse. I did not have time to get out. I went to the lavatory and crouched under the washbasin, pulling the door closed with fingers on its edge.

Someone came into the office, stepping with less caution now. Someone went directly to the desk and opened a drawer, removed something, and laid it on the desk. I couldn't see a thing. I heard the chair creak and the rustle of papers. I breathed sour cleaning rags under the basin, the stink of old wood rotting in a tropical climate. I began to sweat and my legs ached.

That ache had become numbness before the chair creaked again and the drawer traveled forward, then back. Steps went out of the room then, and I opened the door and heard feet through the warehouse. The rear door opened and shut and then there was silence and I was alone again in the dark.

I stepped out and straightened with difficulty, rubbing my legs. As soon as I could walk I opened the drawer again and took out the folder. This time I carried it into the little tea-tasting room from where the beam of a flashlight would not be visible on the street. I laid it on the table and held the flash over the opened folder to study its contents. The first sheet was a letter to Henry Hunter from the New York office of Paradise Teas, signed by Thomas Brittain. I read with quickening excitement as the opening sentence seemed to jump toward my eyes.

> Dear Henry,
>
> Thanks for the Dragon Well. It may take time, since I have to look around for a buyer, but if this goes as planned, there's no limit. I'll expect the first shipment of ten on the 20th, the second and third as per schedule in your previous letter. The family sends warmest regards and—

*Dragon.* Dragon Well!

I flipped that letter and started to read the one beneath it, then the next. They were in order by date, the most recent date on top. Possibly ten minutes passed. I forgot time. I was completely absorbed.

Light flooded the room. I whirled as I heard, "*What are you doing in here?*"

It was Jean Hunter, fury in her eyes and contempt harsh in the voice with which she challenged me. She stood with one hand still on the light switch. In the other hand she held a gun.

I stood rigid. What answer was there? None but the truth.

"I'm looking through this correspondence file."

"That is obvious." She snatched it and backed to the door again. "I thought you were up to something when we caught you at Uncle Henry's desk. You and your research!" She waved the gun. "Walk ahead of me. Into the office. I'm going to call the police."

But when I saw how hesitantly she reached for the telephone on her uncle's desk, I decided she was bluffing.

"What can you tell the police?" I demanded, feeling bolder. "I came in with my own key, given to me today. It is not unlawful to enter an office where you are employed in order to work overtime."

She clutched the instrument but did not lift it.

I added then, significantly, "Besides, are you sure you want publicity? Your uncle may not like it."

She let go of the telephone. She flipped the folder open and glanced at its contents. "Nothing is missing, apparently. But"—she held out her hand—"I want that key."

My usefulness here was at an end. I gave it to her.

She marched me to the door and said, "Don't come here tomorrow—or any other day again. I'll tell Uncle Henry you have decided not to write that wonderful book about the tea business. If you know what's good for you, that's exactly what you will decide. Now, get out!"

I left then, in a hurry, for I had begun to shake. And I didn't want that girl to see how frightened I was—or how ashamed.

## CHAPTER TEN

THE FOLLOWING DAY, incredibly, Lily and I were aboard a mainland-bound stratocruiser, sitting with heads together and planning what we would do when we reached New York. I had been able to give a legitimate reason for going. Publication of my book had been delayed because of the filming; now a date was announced and the publishers wanted me to appear at a cocktail party. I explained this to Henry Hunter by telephone, regretting the cablegram which precipitated my departure.

Our decision to go was reached after much thought. Lily was still not certain whether leaving Honolulu had been wise.

She had come home from Ing's place at three in the morning and had barely stepped inside the house before I began excitedly to tell her what had happened. She said, "Make some tea, will you? Then we can talk."

I carried the tray to her bedroom. Lily had taken off the jewelry and gold sandals. Her frock, about big enough to fit a ten-year-old, dangled from a hanger. She turned from her dressing table to take the cup I handed her.

"So, it is Dragon Well tea that we are looking for."

"I didn't have time to read all the stuff in that file. But I saw no mention of a tea called Tiger. I suppose there is one. Why," I demanded, "do Chinese have to use such outlandish names?"

Outlandish. I caught myself on that as soon as it was said. Something apart from one's own land—foreign. My father had reminded me often that the words foreign and inferior are not synonymous.

"There is a logical reason for every Chinese name," Lily told me absently. "And—Tiger"—she closed her eyes for an instant—"Yao wrote the character for Tiger in answer to my question about who had attacked him."

She said over her cup, "Tiger—there's something I have been trying to remember—the difficulty is that I think in English and not Chinese. I am too far from China." She shrugged and sipped hot tea. "It may come later. Perhaps not. We have enough to worry about at this moment. When did Thomas Brittain say he expected the first shipment of Dragon Well?"

"On the twentieth."

"But that was yesterday!" She set down her cup and went to put in a call to New York. The telephone company must love us, for we often pay more in one month than the average family spends for a year's service. While Lily was at the phone I undressed, knowing it would be useless to listen, since I wouldn't understand a word. When the connection was made she talked for a long time.

"Was that your father?" I asked, coming into the living room in my nightgown.

"No. I talked to Bill Char."

Bill is her cousin. He is a junior partner in a Manhattan law firm.

"What did you say to him?"

"I told him that Thomas Brittain had just imported ten chests of Dragon Well tea, which probably arrived yesterday. I suggested that he try to find out what Mr. Brittain is doing with those ten chests. I also told Bill to expect your arrival in New York soon."

"But I wasn't planning—"

"I know you weren't. But you decided to come into this with me. Now you are in." She smiled as she added, "You said just the other day that you would like to make a trip to the mainland."

"How about the Waikiki Widow?" I asked, remembering that

Lily had taken her to the Ings' house. "Did you find out anything more?"

"Only that she has a very bad case of gambling fever. Tonight we played poker."

"What did Henry Hunter do—get drunk again?"

"He played with us. He was bored. He lost two hundred dollars."

"Did Blanche Carleton lose money?"

"She won six hundred. She is a shrewd poker player."

The Waikiki Widow was not Lily's chief interest at that moment. Lily lay on the *k'ang,* studying the silk and teakwood lantern which hangs from our ceiling. I went to the window wall and looked out at indigo sky and the dark leaves of the mango tree which fanned in the night breeze. I thought of Henry Hunter and wondered if he was sleeping on pastel satin beside the blonde. My mind wandered to the bed he had shared with the pious Agnes—those sheets had probably been unbleached muslin . . .

Lily started for her room. "I am going out again, Janice."

What on earth . . . ? I followed and stood in the doorway. Lily explained, as she buttoned a white silk blouse, "Tonight Mr. Ing mentioned someone who knew Madame Li's family in China, a man who has reason to be grateful to her father. I didn't have a chance to ask questions, but the longer I think of it the more I feel—" She ducked into the closet and came out with a pair of sharkskin slacks. "If I can meet this man I may be able to persuade him to help us. We need help."

"Why not ask the Chuns?"

"Harry and Ethel have professional reputations to consider. I prefer not to involve them."

"Where is this man?"

"He comes from Java, but from the way Mr. Ing spoke I had the impression that he is now somewhere on the mainland. If that is so, I had better go to New York. My father has many contacts—perhaps through them I can locate this man."

"Then why should I have to go? You can accomplish more than I—this whole business is Chinese."

"Don't forget Thomas Brittain," she said. "Just because he makes a profit from the East does not make him friendly to Orientals."

"So I'll be the go-between."

"Yes. And that is typical Chinese procedure. Good night—don't wait up for me."

The next morning Lily told me that Steve Dugan had got space for us on an afternoon clipper. The rest of the day we were so rushed with packing and last-minute errands that we had no time to talk.

But eventually we were roaring through space with nothing to look at but a sea of white clouds beneath us and nothing to do but sit. Lily told me then that she had learned from the Ings that the man she wanted to see was in one of three places: Seattle, San Francisco, or New York.

"What is his name?"

"Hartford Tseng."

"Hartford? How did he get a name like that?"

"He was educated by missionaries who came from Hartford, Connecticut."

"Where did he know Madame Li's family?"

"You remember that her father was an official in the Dowager Empress's court? Tseng was a palace slave. He ran away and was caught. Her father intervened just before his execution and persuaded the Empress to let the boy—he was sixteen years old—have his freedom. Then he arranged for Tseng to live with the missionary family as a servant. Later Tseng went to Java and became a rice grower. He is in his sixties now, and very rich."

"I thought this whole business was supposed to be so hush-hush," I said. "How did the Ings happen to bring it up?"

"They read local papers too," she said. "They saw the news story of Madame Li's arrival, and they know my Chinese name because they know Gogo Leung. When we first appeared at their house they were puzzled. But after I brought Blanche Carleton the second time, they knew I had some special reason for associating with her. Mr. Ing told me a couple of interesting things. One is that Lady Blanche knew Hollis Knight in Hong Kong, the other is that he obtains merchandise there on the black market. They resent the fact that he is making a profit from the destitution of Chinese refugees."

"He bought the Dragon Well from a refugee," I said. "That's what he told Henry Hunter when he offered it to him."

"You found that out from the Brittain file?"

"Yes. Henry sends weekly reports to New York. In one of them he mentioned that he had been offered thirty chests of Dragon Well tea at a low price. Hollis Knight had got it from someone who smuggled the tea from Hangchow. That's where the Lis were living, isn't it?"

"Yes. What was Mr. Brittain's comment?"

"He sent a cable ordering Henry to buy the tea. I told you that last night."

"Yes, but you were excited at the time. I wanted to be sure of the order in which this happened. First, Hollis Knight suggested to Henry that he might buy the tea—right?"

"Right. Henry wasn't interested because the firm doesn't handle fancy teas. He mentioned it casually to Thomas Brittain as part of his report."

"And Thomas Brittain's answer was a cable ordering him to buy the tea," she said slowly, "and to have it forwarded to New York."

"Not forwarded," I corrected. "Transshipped."

"Why do you make that distinction?"

"Because," I said, "the tea had to be opened in Honolulu first."

"What? Are you sure of that?"

"Positive."

"Why?"

"Because of the law governing imports. Honolulu was the first American port of entry for that tea. It had to go through the tea examiner's inspection before it was delivered to Henry Hunter's warehouse."

"You didn't tell me about the tea examiner," Lily accused.

I felt guilty, so I was on the defensive. "I told you so much. This was one of those details of the business which I was learning."

"Please explain. Where is the tea opened?"

"In the tea examiner's office. He uses some kind of a gadget—it's hard to describe—something like an apple corer. He jabs it into the chest and brings out a sample which is tested for quality. All tea has to be up to certain government standards. Then the chests are sent to the importer, and the tea-taster—Henry Hunter—puts it to another test. Jean Hunter told me definitely that nothing comes into that warehouse which is not tested by her uncle. That's where the monkey business was going on, Lily. They locked the door and I never had a chance to see what he was doing."

"Henry Hunter," she repeated. "I have taken for granted that he is merely a cat's-paw. One should never be so certain of anything without proof. I was relying on intuition, not facts."

Lily leaned back against her seat and withdrew to her own thoughts. After a while I said, uncomfortably, "If we've made a mistake in leaving Honolulu, it's my fault. I should have taken time as soon as I came home from the office to tell you everything I learned. But I didn't know I'd be forced out so soon. And last night a lot of things happened, very fast. We were in a hurry to get to Blanche's house by seven, and I was worried, too, over having to go back to that place alone . . ."

"Stop reproaching yourself," she said. "We have both been in a hurry. What has been foremost in my mind is the pearls. They are small, easily disposed of, and it seemed—it still seems—urgent to find them as soon as possible."

"I wish," I went on, wallowing in regret, "that I'd been more cautious in the office. I might have had time to read everything in that folder. But after someone came in and went out again I felt there wasn't any need to be so careful. Who do you think that was? Jean Hunter? She was suspicious from the first. I think she simply set a trap for me."

"And you walked into it? Possibly. We have no way of finding out who came into that office. There are enough tangibles to consider. We must concentrate on those."

I subsided, grateful for Lily's cool logic.

She said, "It is too late now to worry about having left Honolulu. Tomorrow we will be in New York. We must make careful plans."

Those plans, some discarded after much consideration, others mentioned tentatively, developed and elaborated and repeated many times, occupied us for the rest of the flight. We had breakfast in California, then boarded the transcontinental plane which meant more hours of immobility, until we saw with relief the towers of Manhattan and settled on the runway at La Guardia.

We stepped into an icily brilliant night. I shivered in my cashmere coat. The jacket of Lily's red tweed suit was fur-lined and she didn't seem to feel the cold. We sat on opposite sides of our taxi absorbed in the passing scene: people hurrying past lighted shops and movie houses, the changing pattern from Long Island's boulevards to narrower city streets, columns of modern midtown buildings replaced by squattier, older structures, the bumpiness of Third Avenue under pillars of the elevated, the Bowery, where shabby figures went hunched against the cold, and finally, Chinatown and lights and pungent smells and the nasal, high-pitched sound of Cantonese, and Mott Street, and the doorway to the Wu house.

Then, we were home, and the Wus were greeting us.

First, Lily's father, moonfaced and benign, comfortably rotund in his long gray gown, jet eyes sparkling as he returned the bow of his adored daughter. Then Lily's mother in violet silk, gold and jade pins in her hair, brushing hastily at wet cheeks. I greeted them and was welcomed with affection, while a young whirlwind flung himself at Lily, and Johnny Wu, who will never have the reserve of his elders, cried, "Hey, Lily, hey, this is swell! What did you bring me?"

"Nothing, my greedy brother," she told him, returning his hug.

"Aw, you did too. Come on, Janice—what did she bring?"

"Quiet, incorrigible boy!" commanded his father, while over Johnny's head Lily said, "Lincoln, how are you?" Her second brother answered from the altitude of fifteen-year-old dignity, "Fine. What did you cut bangs for? You look silly."

"Does she perhaps have a sweetheart who prefers a doll-faced girl?" Mrs. Wu sounded hopeful.

"She has a sweetheart," I said, "who would be crazy about her if she looked like a Ubangi."

Lily smiled at her mother. "But there is a Shanghai girl in town now who makes eyes at him. And she's a baby doll. I decided to meet competition."

Lily's father tries once in a while to simulate conventional paternal concern because she is not yet married. "Who is this man?" he asked. "Is he an American? I hope so."

"He is not an American by birth," Lily told him. "His people come from Macao. Do not look so distressed, my father. I have no intention of marrying anyone at present."

Mrs. Wu sighed. "Your rooms are ready and there is just about time to change. Cook says we will eat soon."

Bill Char arrived after dinner. The first thing he asked was, "How is Madame Li?"

"Vitamin shots and plasma have helped," Mr. Wu told him. "She will soon be strong enough for the first operation. If the graft is successful, she may walk again."

Bill nodded, his face devoid of expression. Then he sat down and took a notebook from his pocket.

"About Brittain. I have information from several sources. Paradise Teas has two rooms on Worth Street, one occupied by a part-time stenographer, the other by Thomas Brittain. Crummy offices seem to be customary in the tea business. The family lives on East Fiftieth in a three-story brownstone which they have owned for twenty years. The elder Brittain retired recently and turned the business over to his son. He and his wife are in Florida. This son, Tom, was with the occupation forces in Germany and received his discharge last spring. He is thirty-two years old and a graduate of Harvard Business."

"Is he married?" I asked.

"No. And no steady girl. Apparently absorbed in the tea business. One of our investigators went to his office and found the shipment you mentioned: ten chests wrapped in matting and marked with Chinese characters. At my request Joe Wing called on Brittain the same day with the story that his firm had an order for Dragon Well and he was checking every importer in hope of finding it. Brittain was cagey, but finally admitted he had some. He agreed to sell it to Joe Wing—at a price of eight dollars per pound."

"That is a high price for tea," Lily commented.

"Especially for this tea," her father said sternly. "Mr. Wing delivered it here and we emptied each chest. Nine of them contained Dragon Well—and nothing else. The tenth contained a tea of different quality."

Lily said sharply, "It had been opened?"

"The matting and the metal lining had been cut and patched together again."

"Did you report this to Tom Brittain?"

Bill said, "No. He is being watched. What do you intend to do now?"

"Janice will make the next move," Lily told him. She explained our plan and when she finished Bill rose and said, "Okay. Let's hope it works."

The next day I called Tom Brittain and recited my story, implying, when I told him that I was from an island family, that Henry Hunter was an old friend. He sounded friendly, but reserved.

"I haven't seen Henry since I was a kid," he said. "How is he? Solemn as ever?"

"Since Agnes died, he's very active socially." I added, in the tone with which one makes understatement, "I don't think he goes to church as often as he used to."

I heard Tom Brittain laugh. "His wife said enough prayers in her lifetime to get them both into heaven. It was very nice of you, Miss Cameron, to call and—"

That sounded like a brush-off. I interrupted with: "Oh, but I'm here partly on account of you . . ." and rattled on about the forthcoming novel and my idea for a new book. I finished with the remark that while I regretted having to leave the Honolulu office when I had just begun to learn how it functioned, I hoped now to learn firsthand from the owner about his fascinating business.

He said slowly, "You've caught me at a busy time." Then: "How about lunch? Could you meet me here?"

I could and would.

I saw him waiting at the curb before my taxi reached the building. He was tall, with crisp dark hair, and wore brown tweeds and a russet silk tie. He opened the cab door and said, "Miss Cameron? I'm Tom Brittain. We'd better keep this taxi."

As he seated himself beside me I realized I had expected someone different, possibly a huckster type like Hollis Knight. This was an unexpected dividend. He directed the driver to a restaurant, then turned to me with a smile. I put on my most amiable expression and we regarded each other with mutual interest.

We ate in a wood-paneled tavern which had excellent food. Two Chinese men sat at a table near us. They did not look in our direction. While Tom ordered martinis I excused myself and called Lily from a pay phone. Drinks arrived just as I returned and after we had tasted them he said, "I'm sorry I can't ask you to the house for dinner. My parents would have enjoyed meeting you, but they are out of town. Tell me about this book."

I told him with great enthusiasm. In this version the hero became the owner of the firm. Discussion of it took us through lunch and back to Worth Street. We entered a building with worn marble floors and a creaking elevator. On the sixth floor Tom opened a door which bore the name of the firm. We went through a small anteroom to his office, which had one window facing a sooty neighboring building. The walls were acid green and the furniture was shabby. The room's drabness was relieved by a table covered with containers of gourmet foods: bright little pots of wine-flavored cheeses, bottles of artichoke hearts, brandied fruits, boxes of snails from France, truffles, caviar, and a basket of purple grapes which I thought at first were made of wax.

"They're hothouse grown," he said. "Flown here from Belgium."

He picked up a squatty jar of *foie gras*. "This retails for sixteen dollars. There are a surprising number of people here who think their diet is deficient without it."

On his desk were canisters and color sketches of tea cartons. He tapped one with a forefinger. "I'm struggling with ideas for repackaging. Paradise Teas is getting ready to expand.

"But it's tea importing you want to know about." He pulled a heavy book from a shelf. "I'd suggest you start with Volume I of Ukers. It's the bible of the trade. When you're ready to ask questions I'm at your service."

I took Ukers to a leather sofa where I sat down and began to read, while Tom Brittain went to his desk and studied his sketches.

His telephone rang. I sat with head bent over Ukers' tea dictionary.

"Hello. Oh yes, Mr. Wing, what can I do for you? . . .Not at present . . . You have? . . .Yes, of course. How do you spell his name? . . . W-U? . . . Yes, you can depend on that . . . What? You are certain? . . . In that case, of course, I will give you an immediate refund. And the second lot—you still want that for Mr. Wu? . . . I appreciate your confidence—it was undoubtedly a mistake of the packer. I'll check on it. But it may be a week or ten days before— Y-e-s. That's possible. I can try. I'll let you know. Good-by, Mr. Wing, and thanks."

He hung up and looked at me. I didn't raise my eyes. He swiveled his chair and stared out the window. He swung around and picked up a canister and began to tap the desk with it.

I continued to read: "Agony of the leaves: Tea-taster's expression descriptive of the unfolding of the leaves when boiling water is applied . . . Agony of the leaves: Tea-taster's expression descriptive of the unfolding of the leaves when . . ."

"Wouldn't you rather take that with you?"

I closed the book. "Perhaps I'd better. This is monumental—it'll take days to get through it."

He said good-by with barely concealed relief.

I walked a few feet down the hall, then tiptoed back and opened the door cautiously. In the other room Tom Brittain was talking on the phone again.

"Mac. Something has come up. It's in connection with that Dragon Well. I need your help. I'm going to cable Honolulu to ship by air freight and when it comes, I hope you'll be able to—"

I must have made some kind of move, or else he sensed my presence. He called, "Who's there?" I heard his chair roll back.

I took my wallet from my bag and started into his office, saying breathlessly, "Sorry to bother you again, but when I took out cigarettes my wallet must have—" I went to the sofa, lifted a cushion, and cried, "Here it is!" then turned and waved the wallet at him.

He followed me to the hall without a word. He closed the door on my heels and this time I heard the snap of the lock.

## CHAPTER ELEVEN

FOUR DAYS LATER I went to Tom Brittain's office again. What sent me there was a cablegram which said:

> FOLLOWING YOUR INSTRUCTIONS INVESTED TWENTY BUCKS FOR COPY OF THIS MESSAGE QUOTE DRAGON WELL SHIPPED AIR FREIGHT PAN AMERICAN DUE ARRIVE LA GUARDIA WEDNESDAY THREE PM SPECIAL DELIVERY SAME DAY BY WORLDWIDE TRUCKING AM INVESTIGATING FURTHER HERE SIGNED HENRY HUNTER UNQUOTE

DON'T FORGET YOU OWE ME TWENTY BUCKS AND EXCLUSIVE ON THIS STORY ALOHA STEVE

Bill Char had arranged for the shipment to be watched from the time it left La Guardia until it reached Tom Brittain. When he called to say the tea was being delivered, I started promptly. Lily was scheduled to appear soon after my arrival.

I got off the elevator at the sixth floor carrying Ukers, went briskly down the hall to the door marked "Paradise Teas, Ltd.," opened it and walked in with a breezy, "Hello there. Hope I'm not disturbing you. I just want to exchange this for Volume II."

Tom looked up with a start. He had been reading a letter. The airmail envelope it came in bore a special-delivery stamp. His resentment of my intrusion was so obvious that I turned away to avoid recognizing it.

"Oh!" I exclaimed. "Those are tea chests, aren't they?"

He half rose with effort to be polite. "Yes. A special shipment:" He sat down again and looked at the letter in his hand.

The chests were stacked along the wall. Their matting sides were painted with Chinese characters and I traced one with a finger and babbled, "Just think! This was written in the godown of some Oriental merchant thousands of miles from here!"

So far as I could see none of the chests had been opened.

I persisted. "Do you know what those markings mean?"

"It's the chop, the house name of the exporter." He frowned as I plopped onto the sofa.

"Is this for a local customer?"

"Yes. It will be delivered tomorrow." He gave me a brief smile. "And now, my dear Janice, I'm going to chase you out. I have work to do."

"I'll dash in just a minute. But first, please tell me—"

"Sorry, but I haven't time now." He looked at his watch. "For this order no usual procedures apply, but if you want to know about it I'll tell you later. How about dinner? I'll be through here around eight and—"

The door opened and Lily walked in.

She wore a sable coat and a close-fitting hat of the same dark, soft fur. She had pushed the fringe back and her cameo face wore no makeup other than a light dusting of powder and the scarlet of her mouth. Diamonds glittered at her ears and on the wrist from which she slipped a black suede glove.

Tom rose with a jerk which sent the chair against the window.

When Lily smiled, the room looked more shabby. "How do you do," she said in a fluting voice. "Are you Mr. Brittain?"

I sat quiet on the sofa.

"Yes," Tom said, staring. "Is there something I can do for you?"

He pulled a chair into place for her and she sat down and loosened her coat. Tom's nostrils quivered and I knew he was getting a whiff of Tabac Blonde.

"I am Miss Wu," she said. "Lily Wu. I came to see you about a shipment of Dragon Well."

Tom glanced at the chests. "The tea will be delivered tomorrow, Miss Wu. It only arrived this afternoon."

"That is what Mr. Wing told us. Mr. Brittain, you will do us a very great favor if you will deliver this tea tonight."

He said stiffly, "That is impossible."

"Why?"

"Because—" He hesitated, then went on in a guarded voice, "I haven't received an invoice yet. And I cannot make delivery until I am certain that my shipment is correct. There was a previous error—"

"Yes," Lily said. "Mr. Wing explained."

Relief showed on his face. "There will be no mistake this time. I have made arrangements to have the tea tested. That is why it's impossible to make delivery tonight."

Lily pulled off her other glove. "Mr. Brittain, we appreciate your desire to maintain the integrity of your firm. I am going to request, however, that you do the testing after delivery is made."

"But that's not—"

"This is of great importance to my family."

"I don't understand." His eyes watched her now with suspicion. "Surely a matter of a few hours can't make that much difference."

Lily gave a soft little sigh. "I see that I must tell you why we want the Dragon Well. It is obvious, of course, that there will be no more of this tea available perhaps for years. We were amazed when Mr. Wing told us that your firm was able to get it."

She waited. Tom offered no explanation.

"Perhaps you do not know, Mr. Brittain, that in a Chinese family a birthday, especially of an older person, is a very important event. A relative of ours has a birthday tomorrow. Since this date marks the end of a decade for her we would, even normally, celebrate with a feast. But my aunt has recently arrived from China after being separated from us for many years. She has been ill and has recovered. So tomorrow will be a very special occasion for her.

"She was born in Hangchow. As a child she was familiar with the place called the Garden of the Well of the Dragon because the tea which was grown there was especially fine. My father made inquiries of every importer in New York about the possibility of obtaining Dragon Well for my aunt's birthday celebration. You can perhaps imagine how delighted we were when Mr. Wing told us you had some and that you were willing to sell it to us."

"Did he buy the first shipment for your family?"

"Yes."

"But that is four hundred pounds of tea!"

"There will be five hundred guests. At a Chinese birthday feast gifts are presented to everyone invited. We had hoped to give each a pound of Dragon Well. Now we will give a little less. Each package must be wrapped in paper inscribed with the name of my aunt, her age, the family seal, and customary birthday felicitations. Since the dinner will be given tomorrow night, you can see that there is much to be done before the tea is ready for presentation."

Lily gave him a brilliant smile. "Now you understand the situation. And since other circumstances of this transaction have been unusual, you will undoubtedly not object to a slight deviation from your normal custom."

She was reminding him delicately that a high price had been paid, and no questions asked. If there were other off-color values involved Tom might believe that she was reminding him of those also.

He said, "I was expecting my taster to come here."

"You can change the appointment."

"There are certain utensils used in tea-tasting—"

"They will be provided."

"And the nine chests are heavy—"

*"Nine?* My father contracted to buy ten."

"There are nine chests," he said doggedly.

Lily pulled sable around her shoulders. Not by the quiver of an eyelash did she betray the shock of this information. "Mr. Wing will send someone to pick up the nine chests. May I use your telephone?"

He handed it to her and she dialed a number, then spoke in Mandarin. She set the phone down and told Tom, "The car will be here in fifteen minutes. If you wish to call your tea-taster—"

I rose from the sofa. "This tea-tasting sounds very interesting. Do you think I could possibly come along and watch?"

Tom looked blankly at me. He had completely forgotten my presence. Lily gave me a polite smile. After he had introduced us I said, "I'm doing research for a novel about the tea trade. That's why I'm so eager to see this tasting procedure."

Before he could refuse Lily said, "You are welcome to come with Mr. Brittain. I will go downstairs to meet Mr. Wing's driver now."

We left in two cars. Lily rode in the panel truck which carried the tea chests. I went with Tom.

As we drove toward the Village sleet began to fall and he switched on the windshield wipers. We turned onto Perry Street and I said, "Is this where your tea-taster lives?"

"Yes. Mac works for another firm. This is an extracurricular job for him. He's doing it as a favor."

He stopped in front of an apartment house. A short figure darted toward us and I moved over to let Mr. Mackenzie scramble inside. He flopped beside me and began to brush sleet from his overcoat.

"Excellent timing," he said. "I had just come downstairs." He loosened his woolen scarf, shook it, and wrapped it around his throat again. Tom introduced us and he said, "How do you do? Miserable weather, isn't it? Most disagreeable. Dangerous."

The car skidded to a stop at a red light. He peered through the sleety widow. "Thank goodness there isn't much traffic." He adjusted the scarf so that it covered the side of his head near the glass. "You mustn't mind me. My wife says I'm worse than a prima donna. But in my profession a winter cold—" He shuddered. After a moment he leaned forward and asked Tom, "Did you find out anything?"

"I haven't had any reply. All I know is that the chests got mixed somehow."

"But that's impossi—"

Tom said curtly, "It happened. And I intend to know why. But in the meantime I'm grateful to you, Mac. I don't have any palate—I've found that out—and since this is such a delicate tea—"

"Yes. Not much of it. Dragon Well—I didn't know any was coming out of China."

"We were lucky. This may be the last."

Mr. Mackenzie clasped gloved hands. "A splendid tea. Do you know what crop it is? Never mind. I shall enjoy tasting it again." He asked then, "Are you a connoisseur, Miss Cameron?"

"I'm just a writer, interested in seeing how a tea-taster works."

"This is quite a little treat for me," he confided. "Our firm doesn't import fine teas. I've been tasting nothing but common stuff, for grocery stores and cafes, like—"

"Like Paradise Teas?" Tom said. "Packed in tea bags?"

"Tea bags!" Mr. Mackenzie snorted disdain. Then we were on Mott Street and he looked out the window. "Chinatown. I haven't been there for years. Like another world, isn't it?"

"They drink a lot of tea," Tom said. "And they pay cash."

Lily opened the vermilion door. "Come in, please." She ushered us into the first living room, where her father, dressed in a dark business suit, bowed and said, "How do you do, Mr. Brittain? I am John Wu."

I watched Tom's expression as he stepped onto peach-colored carpet, into the light of silk-shaded lamps with bases of jade and rose quartz. Tom's face was blank with effort not to show surprise. Mr. Mackenzie drew in a sharp breath; he sniffed and murmured, "Sandalwood!"

Mr. Wu said, "Will you come this way, please?"

He led us behind the lacquered screen into the second living room. Most of the furniture had been removed and there was only a long table in the center of the floor with a few chairs. Bill Char was there, and Lincoln Wu. They bowed politely as Lily mentioned our names.

Tom's jaw was set as he asked, "Is the tea here?"

"It will be brought in now."

While Lincoln and Bill carried in the chests, Mr. Mackenzie was at the table making an inventory. An electric plate at one end supported a steaming teakettle. There was a row of small white cups without handles and a chemist's scale which he touched, testing its balance.

Mr. Wu said, "The scale is from my place of business. I am an herbalist."

Mr. Mackenzie nodded. "I will need a spoon, please. And"—he coughed with delicacy—"since, in this procedure some of the social niceties must be dispensed with, a large bowl. One cannot possibly swallow so many mouthfuls of tea."

When the bowl was brought he said, "Good. Now we can begin. Will someone open the chests, please."

While Bill cut matting away, he picked up one of the white cups, saying, "I am accustomed to using Limoges—aah!" The porcelain was almost transparent. He set the cup down gently.

He turned then to Mr. Wu. "Since you are familiar with the scale, will you kindly assist by measuring twenty-nine grains of tea from each chest into these cups? Thank you. I will follow with the boiling water."

When the cups were filled he returned to the first brew and bent over it until his nose almost touched porcelain. He studied "the agony of the leaves" as they unfolded. He looked at his watch, waiting for five minutes to pass. No one moved. The only sound was that of water bubbling in the kettle.

Mr. Mackenzie nodded, took up the glass spoon, dipped it into the first cup, and sucked in a mouthful, held it with eyes closed, then swallowed. He turned to Tom, beaming.

"A splendid tea. I do not remember tasting a Dragon Well of comparable quality. After spending the afternoon with an insipid four-minus restaurant blend, this is delightful." He bent over the second cup.

Tom sighed. He took out a handkerchief and dabbed at his forehead. Then he looked at the teakettle and moved away from its steam. It was not steam which he had wiped from his face.

Finally Mr. Mackenzie turned from the table. "There. We're finished. Except—here's an extra cup. Is there another . . . ?" He looked at the row of chests on the matting-strewn carpet.

"Nine," Tom said.

All the Chinese faces looked toward him. Mr. Wu said, "Mr. Wing placed an order for ten chests of tea."

Tom's voice came out harsh. "Yes. But we received only nine. Our Honolulu office reported one chest damaged."

"Oh," Lily said softly. "That is too bad." She asked, as if it really wasn't very important, "What kind of damage?"

"Water. Some pipes burst in the room above the warehouse."

"And of course," Mr. Mackenzie said, "that means it was ruined. What a shame."

Tom Brittain seemed angry at being forced to make explanation. He said to Mr. Wu, "There was another chest which was improperly labeled. Do you know what Mr. Wing did with it?"

"It is here," Mr. Wu told him. "I thought you might like to verify the mistake yourself."

He nodded at Lincoln, who went out and returned with an opened tea chest which looked identical to those on the floor. Mr. Mackenzie took a handful of dried leaves, sniffed, rolled them on his palm. "Hmmm. I should say"—he glanced at Tom—"that, while this is not Dragon Well, it is an excellent sample of Maloo Mixture." He put the tea back and added, as he dusted his hands, "Sometimes called Resurrection Tea."

If I hadn't been reading the tea dictionary I wouldn't have known what he was telling Tom. Resurrection Tea, Maloo Mixture—in the trade it meant floor sweepings, rubbish. Tom's face was perfectly straight as he said, "Thanks, Mac. I'll take it back and see that it is packaged properly."

Mr. Wu said, "Thank you very much for coming here tonight. You will receive a check tomorrow for nine chests of tea at the price agreed upon."

He bowed to the tea-taster. "We also appreciate your help. Please accept the cups as expression of our gratitude."

The porcelain was more precious than Limoges. Two spots of red came into Mr. Mackenzie's cheeks. He opened his mouth, closed it, then said with dignity, "I shall treasure them."

He cradled the cups in his lap all the way back to Perry Street. I hugged Volume I of Ukers, which felt by then like a slab of granite.

Tom drove with eyes straight ahead and his mouth tight, while in the rear of the car twenty pounds of floor sweepings bumped against his back.

After we took Mr. Mackenzie home Tom headed toward Eighth Street, where he turned to the curbing and stopped. "I'll have to take a rain check on that dinner date. I've got some urgent business to attend to. You won't have any difficulty getting a cab here." He reached across me for the door handle and added, "Sorry, Janice. Can we make it tomorrow night instead?"

"Of course."

When he was out of sight I hailed a taxi and told the driver to take me to Mott Street. I found the family in the midst of discussion. As I joined them Lily said, "All the chests have been emptied. There was nothing in them but tea."

Bill Char added, "And, that shipment went directly from the airport to Brittain's office."

"When I got there he hadn't touched them," I said. "He was reading an airmail letter and he looked furious."

Lily commented, "You had a funny look on your face when they talked about Maloo Mixture."

"Because that was double talk," I explained. "Maloo Mixture means trash—" I jumped from my chair. "Lily! That stuff would never have passed the tea examiner in Honolulu!"

She nodded. "I thought of that also. We had a call just before you returned. Tom Brittain has gone back to his office. Do you know why?"

"I heard him tell Mr. Mackenzie he hadn't received an explanation of the mistake in the first shipment. My bet is that he's cabling Henry Hunter to give him hell."

"I had the impression," Mr. Wu said, "that he lost much face tonight when he had to explain why one chest was missing."

"And now," Lily said thoughtfully, "we can make definite conclusions. The first chest was emptied in the Honolulu warehouse and inferior tea substituted. Of the second shipment one chest was ruined by water—"

"Also in the Honolulu warehouse," I contributed, "by a leak from Hollis Knight's place upstairs."

Lily turned to her cousin. "Bill, I must return to the islands immediately. Can you get space for me?"

"Sure. In this weather you won't have any problem getting a plane out of New York. I'll call someone now about space on the Honolulu clipper." He went into the next room to telephone.

I asked, "Hey, how about me?"

"It seems advisable," Lily said, "for you to stay here a while longer."

"But—"

"I mentioned that call we had just before you returned. We aren't the only ones interested in Tom Brittain. Someone followed you tonight."

I sat down again. "Followed Tom and me?"

"When you left the office a cab was behind his car. Didn't you notice it?"

"No. It was sleeting. Tom had to concentrate on the road. Were we followed here?"

"No, that was prevented. Our man sideswiped the taxi at an intersection a few blocks from Worth Street."

"Who was in it?"

"The passenger showed identification to a traffic officer. All we know is that he is a private detective. The law protects the anonymity of his client."

"In that case, how do you expect me to find out anything?"

"We don't," she reassured me. "But, as our go-between with Tom Brittain, you should keep in touch with him."

"He's taking me to dinner tomorrow."

"Good. And since you are the go-between . . . Mr. Hartford Tseng is now in New York. He has bought Madame Li's pearl for ten thousand dollars. I was planning to see him tomorrow, but now you can go—and deliver the pearl."

Bill returned, saying, "Your plane leaves at midnight, Lily."

She stood up. "There isn't much time. Come along, Janice, and help me pack."

## CHAPTER TWELVE

THE TSENG HOUSE was on Sixty-sixth near Park Avenue. As I walked up to the door I noticed that one of the stones which framed the entrance was scarred where some kind of plate had been removed. It looked like the kind of place which might once have housed an embassy. I found out later that this was the case. Mr. Tseng had owned it for only two years.

Just as I reached for the bell the door opened and a very pretty Chinese girl in a mink coat rushed past me, calling, "Taxi!" to my departing driver. He stopped and she waved and sent me a smile of apology before she got into the cab. It was a far cry, I thought with a smile, from the status of a coolie laboring in rice fields of Java to that of possessor of a Manhattan mansion and a stunning young wife like the one I had just seen.

"Miss Cameron?" The door was being held open by a manservant. "Come in, please. Mr. Tseng is expecting you."

I followed him up a curving marble staircase and along a carpeted passage to a room at the rear of the house. Light filtered through sheer curtains at tall windows, there was a blue Chinese carpet on the floor, carved pearwood furniture, and the air was filled with fragrance from dozens of long-stemmed red roses in porcelain vases on various teak tables.

Mr. Hartford Tseng entered the room and bowed. "Miss Cameron? Very pleased to meet the foster daughter of the Wu family."

He crossed the floor and lowered himself to the center of the pearwood sofa. He shrugged out of a blue crepe jacket lined with squirrel, under which he wore a long Chinese gown of plum-colored silk which must have required yards and yards and yards. I raised fascinated eyes from the bulge of his belly to triple chins, a round face with bright, intelligent eyes, above which his naked brow curved to a completely hairless head. Except that he hadn't the pendulous ears, Mr. Tseng looked startlingly like the Lo Han we have in our house, the old rascal known as the Laughing Buddha.

"I have just finished talking to Mr. Char," he said. "Lily Wu's plane left California an hour ago."

"How did she get space so quickly?"

"Through a Chinese travel agency in San Francisco. They have also made a reservation for you."

I wondered why, when I was supposed to stay here and keep an eye on Tom Brittain. "On which clipper?" I asked.

"You are to sail on the *Lurline,* which leaves San Francisco the day after tomorrow."

I sank onto a chair opposite the sofa, clutching my purse in my lap. "Why?" I said. "I hadn't thought of traveling by ship. It takes so much longer."

Mr. Tseng's bald head bobbed. "That is true. But Thomas Brittain has a cabin reserved on the *Lurline.* He also has space on a Pan American clipper leaving the same day."

"Two reservations?" I said. "That doesn't make sense."

"Whichever transportation he uses," Mr. Tseng told me, "he will have a traveling companion. I shall be on the airplane."

Before I could ask any more questions he put fat hands on his knees and leaned forward. "You have the pearl?"

I opened my purse and handed him the small tissue-wrapped lump. He tore off the paper and tossed it to the floor. Then the pearl glowed in his palm.

His eyes narrowed to slits. He looked at it for a silent moment and then: "From Tz'u Hsi's tomb to Sixty-sixth Street is a gratifyingly long way," he whispered.

He had forgotten me. From the very fat, very rich, very important Mr. Tseng, once slave of the woman who had worn this jewel, such intense emotion emanated that walls seemed momentarily too close.

"Exquisite?" He touched the pearl delicately with one finger. "We must recover the others," he said, and laughed softly.

I shivered in the warm room.

He laid the pearl on a table beside a vase of red roses. He leaned back and clasped dimpled hands over plum-colored silk. His face became a mask of half-stupid, half-malicious humor.

"Perhaps we will meet in Honolulu, Miss Cameron," he told me. "Thank you for coming. When you see Mr. Brittain this evening you are to tell him of your departure. He may not choose to tell you of his plans. Nevertheless, we shall soon find out what the young man intends to do."

That evening Tom took me to dinner at a small French cafe on Fiftieth Street. "Hope this is okay with you," he said as we were seated at a corner table. "I chose this place because they know me here, and I'm expecting a call."

"I'm glad it's quiet enough for us to talk," I said, "since it's the last chance we'll have. I'm leaving in the morning."

Tom cocked an eyebrow at me, but didn't say anything because the waiter was asking what we would like to drink. When the man had gone Tom asked, "Why the sudden departure?"

"I've been called back," I lied. "They're adding a scene to the shooting script and I have to be there."

Our martinis arrived and Tom raised his glass and said, "Let's drink to a reunion in Hawaii. I might be there soon myself."

My heart jumped. "When?"

"I'm not sure. It depends on this call I'm expecting." He set down his glass and asked, "Do you know a fellow there by the name of Knight? We rent the lower floor of his building."

"I've met him. Why?"

"We've got a sort of deal on." He was cautious. "I'm planning to remodel our house and open a restaurant. We're near the United Nations and I think I might develop a good business by specializing in foods of various nationalities. On the second floor I'll have gourmet items, including our teas in fancy packages, displayed in a sort of gift shop. Knight is interested—that's one reason why I want to go. And I've—"

A waiter interrupted. "Telephone, Mr. Brittain." Tom rose hurriedly and went to a booth near the front of the cafe.

He was scowling when he returned. He sat down and said, "That was long distance. I've been calling Honolulu since I left you last night and still haven't been able to reach Hunter. The operator reports that the only answer she gets from his house is 'no stop.' "

"A maid must be answering. That's pidgin for 'not here.' "

Where was Jean Hunter? And the missionary was staying in the Hunter house. One of them should at least speak to the operator.

"Our Honolulu office tells me the same thing," Tom said angrily. "Hunter isn't there."

I could have informed him that he'd probably find Henry at the house of the Waikiki Widow. I said instead, "Do you suppose we might travel together? It would be fun."

"When do you leave California?"

"Day after tomorrow, on the *Lurline* from San Francisco."

"If I go," he said, "I'll arrive before you do. I've got space with Pan American."

His regret at the variance in our plans seemed genuine. Through the balance of the meal we talked about the tea business and then about Hawaii, and although I gave Tom several openings he did not mention his alternative reservation.

Might as well take whatever comes, I admonished myself as I prepared to leave New York. The only thing you're sure of is that you're sailing on the *Lurline*. The trip will either seem short and enjoyable, or long and dull, and there's nothing you can do about it.

As it happened, I was wrong on every count.

## CHAPTER THIRTEEN

I AWOKE TO the steady throb of ship's engines, then lay for a while and listened to comfortable creaking sounds as the *Lurline* plowed her way across the Pacific. I was on A-deck in a single cabin which was one of three opening off a short corridor. My quarters were spacious and light and I was grateful for privacy, so welcome after the fatigue of a transcontinental flight that I had locked my door and gone to bed with a novel immediately after dinner.

Now I was rested and curious to find out which passengers would be island friends or acquaintances. I got out of bed to have a look at the weather before dressing. Mist blew into my face, the world outside was swirling gray, water surged rhythmically against the ship's sides. A wonderful morning for walking. I closed the window and began to dress, humming a lively tune.

Just as I stepped into the passage I heard a scream. The door opposite mine opened and Tom Brittain, in pajama pants, half his face lathered, hurtled down the brief passage, flung open the door of the cabin next to his, and rushed inside.

I followed.

A slim figure staggered out of the shower, gasping. She wore a green rubber bathing cap and she held a bright metal object in her hand. The flesh of her breasts and shoulders was reddened. Steam followed her.

I stood rooted to the threshold behind Tom.

Seeing him, she stopped, then darted to the bed for a thin blue nightgown which she held before her, crying, "Get out of here!"

"Are you hurt?" He made an involuntary gesture with the razor in his hand.

She dropped the object she was holding and it rolled across the carpet. She clutched inadequate blue chiffon against her with both hands. "No, I'm quite all right. It was the shower handle—it came off—" She collapsed onto her unmade bed. *"Will you go, please?"*

I retreated backward until I got around the corner. When I heard Tom's door close again I returned to my cabin and sat down and began to see light where no light had been before.

Among other thoughts which swirled through my mind was the reflection: *Why did I ever think the Waikiki Widow was too thin?*

When I started out again I was not humming any lively island song. I had paused near the shopping center and was making rueful inventory of my wardrobe and wishing they carried clothes in size fourteen, when Tom came striding toward me, fingers still at his tie. He was whistling.

I said, "Good morning, Tom. I thought you'd be on the clipper."

Tom stopped whistling. "My plans were changed unexpectedly." He smiled then, as if remembering that he should be delighted to see me. "But this promises to be a very interesting trip. I was going to look you up after breakfast. Where is your cabin?"

"Just across from yours."

His smile grew broader. "Well, well. Isn't that a coincidence?"

I ignored that and said, "Was she hurt?"

"Who?" He stopped and looked at me. "Oh. Were you there?"

I explained, and finished with: "What happened?"

As we fell into step and headed for the dining room, Tom said, "Our plumbing is back-to-back. I was shaving and heard her turn on the water, then I heard a bump and a scream. The shower handle came off." He could barely keep from grinning. "I hope she wasn't scalded!" The last was fervent.

I looked sideways at him. "I suppose your interest is strictly academic?"

Tom let the grin show. "Not in the least," he admitted. "How's your appetite?"

He ordered an enormous breakfast and chomped heartily while I gnawed toast and choked down a cup of coffee. "Beautiful day, isn't it?" he said.

"There's a thick fog." In more ways than one, you dope.

Tom finished his third cup of coffee and lit a cigarette. He announced, with the air of one who has inside information, "I'm afraid we're due for a rough crossing."

"What gave you that idea?"

"Got it from Pan American. There's a storm forecast. We'll probably hit it tomorrow."

"Probably." I wasn't thinking of the weather.

After breakfast we returned to A-deck and Tom got his briefcase and settled at a desk in the writing room. I sat in the adjoining lounge with a magazine, detesting this game of tagalong, wishing I could see the papers he studied so intently.

About half an hour later a woman entered the lounge, shaking moisture from a white coat and slipping a scarf from her head. She pushed blonde hair from her cheeks, met Tom's eyes and looked startled, then smiled and nodded as she walked past. Tom left the desk and came to my chair. "Do you know that woman who just passed?"

"Yes. She is Lady Blanche Carleton."

A black-haired man in a nearby chair raised his head quickly, then looked back at his newspaper with the intent pose of one who listens.

"Is she from Honolulu?" Tom asked.

"From Hong Kong. She's living now at Waikiki."

I started to mention that Henry Hunter knew her and thought better of it. Tom said, "What were you going to say?"

"Nothing important. Just that I went to a party at her house the night before I left Honolulu."

He looked satisfied. He gathered papers into his briefcase and said, "I have to leave this with the purser. Be a good girl and take care of our table seating, will you?"

When I inquired about seating I found that it had already been arranged for Tom. He was with Lady Blanche. My table was across the room. I made necessary alterations in that little plan and went back to the lounge, a vague idea taking shape in my mind.

The black-haired man was still there. He had shown definite interest in Blanche. What if I did a little maneuvering on my own?

He glanced at me several times. I finally met his eyes and smiled. "I've been making bets with myself," I told him.

"About what?"

"About you. That you're a mining engineer."

"How did you know?"

"Your cufflinks. They're gold nuggets, aren't they?"

He held up a hairy wrist. "Pretty smart. These came from the Philippines."

We began to talk. Eventually he asked the questions I expected and I gave the answers he wanted. When I rose to go he remarked, looking gratified, that he would see me later. I said I hoped so.

Next on the agenda was Blanche Carleton. After I changed for dinner I went to her cabin. She opened the door, smiling, then couldn't quite hide her disappointment. "Janice Cameron. What a surprise!"

"Isn't it?" I said. "May I come in?"

Her cabin was larger than mine or Tom's. Our three were the only ones on that corridor. Someone had made a careful study of the ship's plan before reserving this space. I thanked the Chinatown agency for being equally efficient and sat down. The room looked as if six women had dressed in it. Lingerie over chairs, dressing table littered, shell-pink satin robe tossed on the bed, plus the perfume which already permeated the air, made the place reek of femaleness. And Tom was scheduled to visit her here, remembering what he had first seen . . .

Blanche put down her comb and took the white coat from its hanger. "Let's have a drink, shall we?"

As our heels clicked along the passage I explained my trip to New York, then asked, "But what on earth are you doing aboard?"

"I flew to California on impulse," she confided. "Some friends were passing through and I spent a few days with them, hearing all the news about Sussex. One grows quite dreadfully homesick, you know."

You liar, I thought. You hated Sussex as much as your husband's family detested you.

Tom Brittain caught up with us at the entrance to the bar. He said warmly, one eye on Blanche, "Thought you might be here."

We took a corner table. Tom helped Blanche remove her coat and I saw that she was wearing black chiffon. The strapless slip under it was cut very low.

When Tom sat down he had that silly look on his face again.

Blanche was smiling. "You did not recognize me earlier today?"

"You had too many clothes on. I'm glad to see that you weren't seriously burned." His laughter joined with hers, while I sat and looked pleasant until my face ached.

That night Dan Gordon appeared.

Tom had gone for cigarettes and as Blanche and I chatted I saw a heavy-set man dinner clothes stop in the doorway to survey the room. His glance met mine and he started toward us immediately.

"Hello. Remember me? I'm Dan Gordon. We met in the lounge." He turned to Blanche. "And you're Lady Blanche Carleton. We were at a party together about a year ago."

Blanche had stiffened. He went on, "In Macao, at the Havana Hotel. We all wound up in the fan-tan rooms on the top floor. May I join you?"

When Tom returned he glared at the man who occupied his chair. Blanche gave the slightest shrug as she said, "Do sit down. This is Mr. Gordon"—she turned to the interloper—"from Manila, aren't you?"

"Right."

They shook hands and Tom looked startled when Gordon said, "In the tea business, aren't you? Thought I recognized the name when I saw it on the passenger list."

"I didn't—" Tom began, and changed it to, "You mean the ship's list?"

"No, in the Matson office."

There was an odd silence. I looked at my glass while I considered this information and wondered what Tom would say. Tom said nothing. Blanche might have mentioned at that point that she also knew someone in the tea business, but she did not.

Gordon grinned. "Looks like this trip's going to be tolerable after all. What're you drinking, scotch? Steward!"

The four of us walked in to dinner together. Gordon, of course, was at our table. The last two chairs were occupied by a couple named Fentriss, who said they were making the two weeks' cruise. Harry Fentriss was thin and sallow, inclined to be morose about the high cost of production in the automobile industry and the lousy climate of Detroit. His wife, slightly haggard in a red dinner dress, informed us that it was their first sea voyage, they'd both been sick, and she wished we'd get into some tropical sunshine.

When she heard Blanche's name she brightened and became increasingly effusive as we drank the wine Gordon ordered for our table. We adjourned in a body and when dancing started we were still together. Tom led Blanche to the floor first and I danced with Dan Gordon, who held me too tight against a barrel chest. He said, "How'm I doing?"

Wishing he were a bit more subtle, I answered, "Fine. Did you really meet her in Macao?"

"Nope. But she was too high the night I saw her there to remember anything. I did meet her husband—"

"On the same party?"

"No, in Shanghai. Stuffy old coot. Don't blame her for busting loose when she can. Where's he now—seasick?"

"He's dead."

"O-o-h." He looked thoughtful. Then he said, "Look at your friend."

Tom and Blanche were near us. Tom's face was flushed. He was asking something to which she gave a smile and a nod of assent.

Gordon said, "Better call up the reserves, girl."

"What can. I do?"

"This is the kind of detail I like." He chuckled. "You just watch the maneuver."

We sat down and a steward brought a pinch bottle and some setups. Gordon mixed drinks and announced, "This is my last taste of civilization. I've got to make the most of it."

Dorothy Fentriss protested, "But our travel agent said Manila is very gay now."

"Bah!" Gordon drank without a chaser. "Got a big house staffed with servants and I never stay there. Spend most of my time in camp, it's not so lonely. There's a shortage of women in Manila. I try to get away every six months—used to fly to Shanghai. Now it's Hong Kong or Macao, but they're jammed with refugees."

He looked at Blanche. "Bet you were mighty glad to leave." She smiled and reached for her purse with a gesture of withdrawal. Gordon's eyes narrowed. He said quickly, "Speaking of refugees—I picked up something recently—you women might like to see it." He dropped a ring on the table, a thin platinum circle set with a marquise diamond.

Dorothy Fentriss squealed, "Oh, look at that, Harry!"

Her husband picked it up. "It's a beauty," he said, squinting. "About four carats, eh? How much did it set you back, Gordon?"

Gordon shrugged. "About half what it's worth." He looked at Blanche. She was rigid, eyes on the stone. "Try it on," he suggested. When she didn't move he picked up her hand and slipped the ring on her finger. "Might have been made for you."

The orchestra began to play and he said, "Let's dance." She started toward the floor, sending Tom a brief glance over her shoulder.

Tom said abruptly, "Excuse me. I have some work to do." When I passed the lounge later I saw him sprawled in a chair, staring at his toes. Score one for Gordon.

The next night we were the usual party. Tom's attitude toward Blanche was as attentive as before, while she showed no overt preference either for him or Gordon. At ten she said good night, mentioning a headache. Tom made a little pretense of interest after that and soon excused himself. Gordon scowled at his retreating back and I thought: Tom's trick this time. Then Gordon left. The Fentrisses exchanged glances.

"Hadn't we better . . . ?" I said, and the party broke up.

Which bed was Blanche in? No sound from her cabin or Tom's. Gordon had mentioned that he paid extra fare to be alone in a double stateroom on B-deck. I strolled in that direction. A steward passed, delivering a bottle and two glasses to Gordon's room. I returned to my cabin. A few minutes later the door opposite mine slammed. Tom, I decided, was going, to have a restless night.

I wondered, the following evening, how the contest would go.

There was a movie scheduled, and as we left the dining room Gordon said, "How about a little poker until the dancing starts? Had a losing streak in San Francisco—my luck wants to turn."

"Oh, let's!" Dorothy Fentriss cried.

"It might be amusing," Blanche said languidly. Her eyes went to Tom. "For a little while."

We went to Gordon's stateroom where he ordered a table set up. I wanted to play, but decided it was more advisable to watch, and pulled a chair alongside Tom. He won the first round of draw with a pair of queens. The pot was eighty dollars.

This was going to be interesting.

They were all good players. Gordon held cards casually, a glass at his elbow. Harry Fentriss also drank, and his wife chain-smoked, looking ten years older as she studied her hand. Blanche's face was pale and she seemed remote, hardly speaking except to ask for cards or make a bet. Tom was lucky at first—in an hour he won two hundred dollars, then dropped most of it. The atmosphere grew more tense. Conversation came to a stop.

When the orchestra began to play, Tom looked at Blanche, but she ignored him. Gordon dealt stud and Blanche won with three sevens, one in the hole. It was a big pot. Dorothy's eyes began to grow bloodshot; the ashtray beside her overflowed with smoking cigarette butts. No one seemed to be aware of it, but the pattern of the game was obvious by then—every time Dan Gordon held the deal Blanche won.

I decided to collect ashtrays. A smoldering cigarette dropped and I went on my knees to pick it up. I froze there, staring at Blanche's legs under the table. Then I rose and emptied the ashtrays and sat down again beside Tom. Gordon was dealing stud. Tom lit a cigarette and when he set it down I contrived to knock it off and kick it under the table.

"Oh," I said. "Tom, your cigarette—"

He bent absently, couldn't reach it, he went down on one knee as I had done. He fumbled for quite a while, and I knew what he was looking at.

Blanche was wearing a white lace dress with a tight slip, which had pulled up so that her legs were silhouetted through lace. On the inside of one knee was a dark purple bruise, in a design which could only have been made by a human hand.

Tom returned to his chair and placed the cigarette carefully on the tray. Gordon held the deck, waiting. Tom glanced at his hole card and nodded. Gordon dealt to him and then on around. Blanche won that hand, and the next. Gordon refilled the Fentriss glasses.

When his chips were gone Tom said, "Deal me out for a while. I want to get some air." I followed him. We stood at the railing watching whitecaps and feeling wind in our faces. He said, "Do you know what section of San Francisco has a Seabright exchange?"

"No. Why?"

"It's not important. What does matter is that in the phone book Pan American ticket offices have a Garfield number."

"Tom," I said, facing him. "I don't know what you're talking about."

He hesitated, then said abruptly, "Come to my cabin. I want to show you something."

What he showed me was a note on a Pan American memo pad which said:

> Dear Mr. Brittain:
>
> Will you kindly telephone Miss Parker immediately in regard to your reservation?

A number with a Seabright prefix followed.

Tom's eyes never left my face while I read the note. I laid it down and shrugged and asked, "What does it mean?"

He said, still watching me, "I had been in my hotel in San Francisco less than an hour when this note arrived by messenger. I called the number and spoke to Miss Parker. She told me I'd been off-loaded from the clipper because of military priority. When I asked about later space she said there were storm warnings over the Pacific and flights were being canceled. As a favor to me, Pan American had reserved a cabin on the *Lurline,* sailing that same day at four o'clock. That's how I happened to be aboard."

He was still studying my reaction. I looked directly at him and said, "That's all too deep for me."

"I'm over my head too," he said. "But I can swim."

I wanted to say a lot of things then. I said good night.

## CHAPTER FOURTEEN

ON THE LAST NIGHT we wore paper hats and were very gay. Blanche appeared wearing ice-blue-satin—and the marquise diamond. When she caught me looking at it she held out her hand. "I was frightfully lucky after you left last night."

Gordon sent Tom a smile. "Don't ever play showdown at the end of a winning streak."

Tom said smoothly, "I never do. That's for suckers:" He turned to Blanche. "Lovely lady, would you care to foxtrot?"

I danced with Gordon. "Are you staying long in Honolulu?"

"About six hours."

"Where will you spend them—Waikiki?"

"That's not for me, honey. I'm driving Lady Blanche around the island. Might persuade her to make a trip to Manila before she goes home."

I said confidentially, "Rumor has it that the lady doesn't care much for England. Don't be disappointed it she says no at first. Give her your address."

"I'm way ahead of you," he said. "She already has it."

We went back to the table. Tom partnered Dorothy Fentriss next and when they returned from their dance she seemed about to purr. He informed me, when my turn came, that I was the most stimulating girl he had ever known.

"Is that what you told Dorothy?"

"No. She's the most beautiful."

"And Blanche?"

"The most fascinating."

"And the best poker player?" I couldn't resist that.

Tom grinned at me. "Indubitably." Then he took us into a series of gyrations which prevented further conversation.

He carried on like that for hours. I couldn't figure his behavior. Was he as smitten with Blanche as he acted? Or was he drinking so much to drown his humiliation at Gordon's success, the token of which she wore on her hand? Under Tom's antics I thought I perceived mounting tension as the *Lurline* bore us steadily nearer Honolulu. Whatever his reasons, he was the gayest among us. At two o clock Harry Fentriss helped him to bed.

He didn't appear for breakfast. I went to his cabin and, when he failed to answer my knock, I walked in and found him asleep.

"Wake up, Tom. We go ashore soon."

He sat with head in his hands. "I wish I hadn't cabled Hunter. I'm in no shape for a welcoming committee."

"Maybe this will help." I handed him aspirin and water.

While he took it I refrained from informing him that he was apparently not getting the traditional island welcome. When the tugs came to meet us off port, loaded with islanders bearing leis, I had looked for Henry Hunter but failed to find him. I thought that he might have sent his niece, but she did not appear.

Nor was Lily in evidence. She had sent a Chinese girl I had not met before, Orchid Tseng. Orchid was in my cabin now.

I said to Tom, "It's hot in here. See you on deck when you're ready."

He appeared eventually, carrying his briefcase. He wore two leis around his neck. "I see you've been officially welcomed," I commented.

Tom touched gardenias. "The office probably sent these. Blanche gave me the pink ones."

We went to the rail to watch the crowds and listen to the music. Tom said, "Keep an eye out for Hunter. I've almost forgotten what he looks like."

"He's stout and bald. A gold crown shows when he smiles." I watched for Henry Hunter. But he did not appear. No one from Paradise Teas showed, except . . .

One slender figure. Jean Hunter, straining toward the gangplank, grasping the barrier behind which she stood. Her eyes shifted past Tom. She didn't see me. Jean was looking for someone else. When we stepped ashore she was gone. I held out my hand. "So long, Tom."

"Have a good time tonight." He sounded wistful. "I'll bet Blanche throws a terrific party."

I hadn't been invited to any party. "Aren't you going?" I hedged.

"Hunter probably has something cooked up. I'll call you soon."

At the sidewalk I turned to look back. Tom stood alone in the shed. He looked hot, puzzled, and angry.

"Here we are, Miss Cameron." The girl who called from a taxi was Orchid Tseng. Seated beside her was her sister, Jasmine. Both looked young and smartly dressed and frivolous. As we crawled through traffic the girls reported their activities on the *Lurline*.

"I trailed around after Tom Brittain," Jasmine said. "Good-looking, isn't he? I love big men!"

Orchid nudged her and she went on. "After you left, he went to the purser for a briefcase which he took to his cabin. Then a steward paged him and I followed him back to the purser's window, where he picked up a flower box which had been sent out on the tug. There was a gardenia lei inside. He looked puzzled at the card, and when he threw it away I picked it up. It was blank."

Orchid began, "Your cabin door was half open, so I could see very well. As soon as he left the second time, Lady Blanche came out of her cabin. A man in a Palm Beach suit was with her. She called him Hollis."

Hollis Knight had come on the tug, then, to meet Blanche.

"She took something into Mr. Brittain's room while he stood guard outside. When she came out and handed him a manila folder, he left. Then Mr. Brittain returned with a flower box in his hand. He knocked on her door."

"Is that all?"

"I went out on deck and stood near her window. She was calling him 'darling' and talking about a party at her house. He told her he couldn't come—he had to spend the evening with friends of his family."

"What then?"

"I couldn't hear any more talk, so I looked in the window. They were kissing."

Orchid looked at her sister. "Wow!" Both girls giggled all the way home.

Shizu welcomed me and said that Lily was in the garden. I went to the balcony and called to her and she looked up and smiled. "*Aloha nui loa*. Shall I come up?"

"I'll be down. As soon as I can shed some clothes."

I found grass slippers and a kimono and went outside, grateful for the cool and fragrant air. I lit a cigarette and sprawled in a chair by Lily and began to tell her about the crossing. When I finished she said thoughtfully, "That is most interesting."

"What do you mean by 'that'? Blanche's act with the shower?"

"No. I expected something of the sort when I heard that she was aboard. What interests me is the man named Gordon."

"Lily," I said, "his being there was purely accidental. Gordon can't possibly have anything to do with this—"

"Of course not. But the night of the poker game—the bruise an her leg—are you sure it wasn't there before?"

"Positive. Her skin is very white and the bruise was dark purple. I would certainly have noticed it when she came out of the shower."

"So this bruise was acquired after she had spent some time, presumably, in Gordon's cabin."

"Why are you so pleased?"

She said, "Tell me, what do you think of Tom Brittain by now?"

"I like him," I said. "And he's no dope."

"You consider him too intelligent to be made a fool of by a woman like Blanche?"

"That's it. He played along—but with his eyes wide open."

"What do you think he will do now?"

"Nobody met him at shipside. Jean Hunter was watching the gangplank, but not for him. Hollis Knight met Blanche in her cabin, and then ducked out of sight. Henry Hunter never showed at all. He will regret that when Tom gets to the office."

"Tom Brittain won't find him there," Lily said.

"Why?"

"Henry Hunter has disappeared."

"When?"

"He was at the office when the second shipment of Dragon Well arrived. He has not been seen since."

"Did he leave with Blanche?"

"No. Blanche Carleton flew to San Francisco two days before Henry Hunter disappeared. I thought at first that he had followed her. I asked Steve to check local passenger lists, and Henry

Hunter was not on any outgoing ship or plane."

I had been resentful of having to spend those days playing follow-the-leader with Tom and Blanche. But at least we had been doing something. I said, "And you've been here alone, completely stymied."

"Not completely," Lily said. "We now have allies. Eight of them, in fact. And they are very busy."

"Those girls—Orchid and Jasmine—are they Mr. Tseng's daughters?"

"Yes," she said. "They are quite an unusual—"

She didn't finish because a car had stopped in front of our gate. Two Chinese girls appeared on the path: a plump little one in a blue cotton uniform, a taller one in a red seersucker suit. Lily said, "Janice, this is Poppy Tseng. And her sister, Violet."

"Hello," they said in unison. Poppy announced, "We haven't much time. The boss allows half an hour for lunch." She held out a manila folder. "He brought this back from the *Lurline.* I snitched it off his desk."

Lily opened the folder, glanced at the contents and said, "Tom Brittain's correspondence."

I asked Poppy, "Is Hollis Knight your boss?"

"Yes. And he's a stinker. He has a system of hiring girls as apprentices at half pay. As soon as they learn the work he fires them and hires another crew. I'm quite stupid, so it's taking me a long time to learn."

"What do you do?"

"We operate sewing machines. Mr. Knight salvages discarded matting from downstairs. Somebody cuts it into rectangles and we sew tape around the edges. Another crew paints the mats with hula girls. He sells them in curio stores for three dollars."

Violet Tseng said, "I work downstairs as a tea packer. We have half an hour for lunch today too. A shipment arrived yesterday and we have to finish packing it by tonight. Miss Hunter is in a tizzy. Mr. Brittain showed up a while ago and there was a terrific row." She laughed merrily.

"Please," I said. "This suspense is killing me."

Violet perched on a chair arm and lit a cigarette. "Before he arrived he telephoned twice. I heard her tell him that Mr. Hunter was out—he would not be in until tomorrow."

"How could you hear this?"

"She left the door open to be sure we didn't waste time at the packing table. As soon as she hung up on Mr. Brittain, Miss Hunter started trying to reach Lady Blanche Carleton."

I told Lily, "She's driving Dan Gordon around the island. That should take them about five hours."

Lily asked Violet, "What happened when Tom Brittain arrived?"

"Jean Hunter met him in the reception room. She said she didn't know anything about his arrival. When he wanted to go inside she asked for identification. He said he had plenty, and opened his briefcase." She whistled. "Was he mad! They heard him yelling all the way back in the warehouse!"

"What was in the briefcase?"

"Newspapers."

This hadn't helped his hangover any, I thought. "Go on."

"That's all. Jean Hunter came back in the office and closed the door. Then she started calling Lady Blanche again."

Inside the house the telephone rang, and Shizu came to the balcony and called Lily.

"We'd better go," Poppy said.

"Yes, we'd better," echoed Violet. "Our taxi's waiting."

I walked to the gate with them.

"Were those two girls your sisters?" I asked. "The ones who met me off port this morning?"

"Yes," they said simultaneously.

"You don't look like twins," I hinted. Two pairs of bright black eyes turned to me. Two red mouths curved in mischievous smiles. "But you're all about the same age, aren't you?"

Violet said, on a ripple of laughter, "Three of us are seventeen—"

"Three . . . ?"

"Two of us are eighteen," Poppy added. "The last two are fifteen." The taxi, driver started his motor. "Good-by," they chimed. "See you later."

Lily was on the chaise again. I said, "Mr. Tseng must have a lot of wives. Did he bring them all to America?"

"He brought no wives," she said. "He has never been married."

I gaped. Before I could get words out she announced, "That call was from Bena Tseng. She says—"

"Wait, Lily!" I cried. "Could Bena be a diminutive, by any chance, for Verbena?"

"Yes. And if Blanche Carleton is traveling around the island, she is being followed by Iris."

"Oh, for God's sake! A garden! And how many flowers in the Tseng garden?"

"Seven." Lily's face grew more serious. "You have met their adoptive father. He is a remarkable man."

"Why does he want the pearls?"

"He has a very intimate reason for wanting them recovered. Also, he intends to buy one for each daughter."

"You were going to say something about Bena Tseng. What did she call about?"

"She has been watching Matthew Webster. Bena reported that he has just gone to the house in Waikiki."

"To Blanche's? The missionary?"

This was, somehow, an outrage. I had just finished admitting the physical allure of the blonde, but Matthew Webster—he was an ordained minister. Besides, I amended hastily (shades of Somerset Maugham!), he was a sick man.

"What is he doing there?"

"She does not know. When the gate was opened he said something to the gardener, then went inside."

He went inside, I thought. Then aloud, "The missionary arrived after Madame Li, after the Chinese boy was killed. And that night at her house he said he had never met Blanche in China. She was in Peking and Shanghai. His station was in Ningpo."

"Ningpo," Lily said, "is not such a great distance from Shanghai. You may not approve of this, Janice, but his luggage has been carefully searched."

"By whom?"

"I did it. He has a bundle of old letters dating ten years back, including correspondence from Agnes Hunter, a few gifts for relatives on the mainland, a Bible presented by his students, and a modest supply of clothes."

"How did you get into the house? Isn't he there most of the time?"

"Recently he has made two trips, to Kauai and to Maui, calling on customers of the tea firm. He inquired there for Henry Hunter. He also spends many hours at Waikiki, sunbathing. The Hunter maid has the usual day off. I went when the house was empty."

"So now you've trailed him to the Waikiki Widow. I suppose someone is installed there, too, impersonating a servant."

"I couldn't manage that," Lily said regretfully. "Blanche has been away. The house was closed."

"But it's open now. And I can just picture a white-haired old missionary draped over that zebra-skin bar, guzzling straight gin."

Lily's remote expression indicated that my remark did not amuse her. She picked up the folder and began to read, laying Tom's papers aside as she finished. I took what she discarded and we read in silence.

## CHAPTER FIFTEEN

TOM'S PAPERS confirmed the opinion I had already reached about him. The only additional information we obtained was that a statement from the Bishop Bank, apparently mailed to New York without Henry's knowledge, indicated a discrepancy between one month's income and operating expense in amount of thirty-eight hundred dollars. No wonder Tom was worried.

When we had finished reading Lily said, "You were right. He knows less than we do."

"Then we had better get him told," I said decisively. "He has a right to know."

"I am reluctant," she admitted. "This is probably my wish to exclude a *haole* from a purely Chinese affair."

I put index fingers to outer corners of my eyes and pulled up. "Do I look Chinese now?"

"You are different. You are involved because of our relationship."

"Tom Brittain is involved too. It is his firm which is being used, and his business reputation might be at stake."

"Of course," she said. "And if, as you say, he is aware of Blanche

Carleton's maneuvers, and clever enough to reverse their positions, Tom Brittain can become our key figure."

"That's possible," I said. "Blanche really isn't so smart. She made elaborate arrangements for meeting Tom and arousing his interest, but when another man came along who offered the right bait . . ."

Lily said in a thoughtful voice, "Mr. Tseng has been able to add a few facts to what we previously knew about her. She had an affair in Shanghai with an American, one of Chennault's mercenaries. He was known to have beaten a Chinese girl to death. Since the girl was only a prostitute, it was hushed up—"

"So," I said, "I see now why you were interested in the bruise on her leg. If that's what she prefers, Gordon is the prescription."

Lily said, "You had better call Tom Brittain now. Ask him to come here as soon as possible."

"Okay." I spoke through a yawn. "But I'd rather sleep."

I didn't reach Tom until nine that night. When he finally answered, I heard music in the background. "I'm in the lobby," he explained. "Been sitting on the terrace, watching hula dancers with the Fentrisses."

"Having fun?"

"How could I help it? This is hospitable Hawaii. I'm loaded with aloha."

I hoped he wasn't loaded with anything else. He waited, then said pointedly, "We're just leaving for Blanche's party."

"Fine!" I told him with enthusiasm which I did not feel. "I'll see you there."

The place blazed with lights and vibrated with activity. Musicians stood at the end of the lanai playing something lively, and several couples were dancing while others clustered around the bar. I wandered until I located Tom at a table near the swimming pool. With him were the Fentrisses, Hollis Knight—and Blanche, of course. She sat between Tom and Hollis. Her laugh stopped short when I approached. She didn't get up, and her voice had an edge of anger.

"Janice. What a delightful surprise."

I smiled my prettiest. "I thought at first I couldn't make it. But when Tom insisted . . ." I sat down and said to Hollis, "Hello again. I saw you on board the *Lurline* this morning, carrying flowers."

His mustache twitched. "I went out to meet Lady Blanche."

Tom barely acknowledged my arrival. His eyes didn't seem to focus properly. He blinked at the lighted pool where half a dozen swimmers cavorted around a bobbing table which held a bowl of punch.

"Looks—just—wonderful," he proclaimed. "Very, very enticing."

"Would you like to go in?" Blanche asked.

"With you?"

"I have to play hostess." She glanced toward the lanai. Tom stood up. "Then let's dance."

I watched them. They had taken a few steps when a houseboy spoke to Blanche. She followed him. I made a beeline for Tom and held out my arms. He had to be polite. We circled. Then I asked, "Are you as drunk as you act?"

He said, "I'm cold sober. And I've never been so angry in my life."

I let out a breath of relief. "What did that houseboy tell her?"

"She had a visitor. In the library, wherever that is."

"Thank God you're sober," I said. "Let's see if we can find out who that visitor is." I started into the house, pulling Tom with me.

"What—" he began, and I jerked his arm, saying, "Be quiet."

The door of the library was shut, but we heard an excited voice inside. I yanked Tom again and we went out the front and dodged through croton shrubs to the other side of the house. Windows there were closed but the drapes weren't pulled across them. The library was a lighted stage.

Blanche was talking to her visitor, a tall girl in a cotton skirt and blouse—Jean Hunter. Blanche wore blue tulle, and she looked poised and beautiful compared to the pale angry girl. Jean's face was not only bare of makeup, it was smudged with dirt, and she looked tired. Obviously the physical contrast between them was the last thing that concerned her. She was accusing Blanche of something, while Blanche shook her head, smiling, and made a brief remark. This infuriated Jean beyond control and she grasped the other woman by the shoulders and began to shake her.

The door opened and Hollis Knight entered. He went to the two women and tore Jean's hands loose, then held her arms at her sides.

While she struggled, Hollis said something, then propelled her into the hall.

Alone in the room, Blanche went to a mirror and began to smooth her hair. She was smiling.

Tom said, "That's the girl—"

"—who wouldn't let you into your own office today," I said. "And now I know why. Let's get back to the lanai before Blanche does."

We were dancing when she came out. She hesitated at the edge of the floor, then went to greet two couples who were just arriving.

Tom's hand hardened against my back. "Now," he said, "You'd better explain a few things."

"I will, after we get out of here. Try to think of some excuse to leave. It's got to be good."

Tom said, "Once, on the *Lurline,* we talked about swimming. How good are you?"

"I learned from Hawaiians."

"Okay," he said. "Remember, I've been drinking all day. Don't be surprised at what I do."

We started toward the garden. Tom walked unsteadily; I held his arm. At the edge of the swimming pool he said under his breath, "Begin to argue. Try to hold me back." He leaned forward, laughing like an idiot.

I clutched him with both hands. "Tom Brittain, don't you dare . . . !" just as he sprawled into the water, pulling me with him.

We came up threshing, amid exclamations from bystanders and delighted screams of the swimmers. Several people rushed to the pool's rim, Blanche and Hollis Knight among them. Tom sputtered and choked and went under, and I cried, "He can't swim!" and tried to bring him back to the surface. Someone shoved the floating table to us and I pulled Tom up by his lapels and said, "Hold onto it, Tom, for heaven's sake." He clutched the table while I swam one-armed to shallow water towing table and Tom with me.

Out on the lawn again, Tom looked sheepish. I pulled clinging skirts from my legs and snapped, "He needs black coffee." I glared at faces crowding around us. "As for me," I announced, "I'm going home."

"Sorry, Janice," Tom mumbled. "I'll take you."

"I have a car, thanks." I started away. He stumbled after me, insisting stubbornly, "Gotta take you home."

Someone laughed. I quickened my pace, Tom lumbering behind.

Blanche followed us to my car. Tom flopped onto the front seat, then leaned out to catch her hand. "Sorry, lovely. Be back soon's I'm dry." He kept on saying it while I started the motor, backed the car, and headed out of the driveway like a woman too angry for speech.

When we were on the street he straightened. "I owe you a new dress."

"That's all right, Tom. This is nylon. What about your clothes?"

"Drive to the hotel entrance. I'll send a bellhop to my room."

When we were headed toward Tantalus at last, he said, "Now. Do you know what this Grade B scenario is all about?"

"Yes. A lot of it."

"Then start talking."

"Not until we're at the house," I said. "Somebody else has to be in on this. Give me a cigarette, please."

"I'd rather give you a poke in the jaw. Here you are."

Lily opened the door for us. Her brows twitched at sight of Tom's waterlogged white suit, but all she said was, "Come in, Mr. Brittain. It is nice to see you again."

Tom towered over her. He said wryly, "Miss Wu. The pleasure is all mine."

I headed for the hall, saying, "Tom, you can use the bathroom to change. Second door on your left."

When we returned to the living room Lily was setting a tray on the chow bench.

She answered Tom's look with, "I am Janice's foster sister, Mr. Brittain." She seated herself and poised the teapot. "As a tea expert, I presume, you do not take sugar or cream?"

He nodded as he sat down on the *k'ang*. He glanced around the room, noting the moon door, a silk scroll, red ginger on a teakwood table. "This is an improvement over Lovely's little nest at Waikiki."' He turned to me. "And that's as good a starting point as any. Who's paying her rent?"

I bit into an almond cake. "Henry Hunter."

Tom said nothing. I added, "That means, probably, that you are paying it."

He picked up his cup. "Keep on talking, Janice. When you run out of breath your little friend here can take over."

It was after midnight when we finished.

Tom had risen. He stood at the window wall and looked at Honolulu below our hillside, where lights were gradually blinking out at this hour. He said, "I understand a lot of things I couldn't figure before. A feeling I had, for instance, of being followed—"

"A private detective," Lily said, "was employed by Blanche Carleton. She needed to know your movements in order to plan her own."

"She was Miss Parker?"

"Probably. The Seabright number was that of an apartment occupied by a blonde woman. She paid a month's rent and stayed there less than a week."

"Henry must have told her you were suspicious of the tea mix-up," I said. "She took off for the mainland immediately."

"And two days later Hunter disappeared?"

"Yes."

"So she couldn't have—" He seemed relieved.

*"Men!"* I thought. If she had been old, or had a shape like a bag of rice . . .

"Lily, where are Tom's papers?" I asked.

He was startled. "You have them?"

Lily produced the folder. "We recovered these from Hollis Knight."

"And which is *his* little playmate—Blanche or the Hunter girl?"

"Lady Blanche. They knew each other in Hong Kong."

"At the same time," I pointed out, "he seems friendly with Jean Hunter."

"I recognized his type when we met tonight," Tom told us. "He's one of the angle boys. Plays both ends against the middle, always with an eye for a fast buck."

"You said in New York that you had some kind of deal with him," I reminded him. "What is it?"

"I wrote Hunter about my plan to expand the business. Although I didn't think it necessary to explain to him, that was why I wanted the Dragon Well. I had a letter from Knight shortly after that, suggesting that I rent him space in the gift shop. He mentioned some of the stuff he handles and I thought it might fit. All this was tentative."

"It was Hollis Knight," Lily said, "who located the Dragon Well tea in Hong Kong and suggested it to Henry Hunter. Also—did Mr. Hunter ever mention any tea called Tiger?"

"There's no such thing," Tom said promptly. "This guy Knight is an importer. I suppose, with the China boycott, that means he's buying black market stuff."

"He bragged about it," I said. "The Dragon Well was black market tea. Hollis probably took your briefcase because he and Blanche wanted to find out how much you knew—or suspected."

"It was mighty convenient for Hunter's niece," Tom said. "She wouldn't let me into the office today. So they've all found out about me. I'm ignorant—and gullible." He snapped the folder shut. "What do we do now?"

"I have keys to your warehouse," Lily said, "and to the factory upstairs. We might learn something by going there. If we are challenged, you have a right to be in the building at any hour." She looked at him and waited for consent.

Tom hesitated. "There's one more point I'd like to get cleared. Why haven't you reported any of this to the police? It isn't by any chance because you *prefer* to have these pearls smuggled into the country?"

Lily's chin went up. She rose and went to stand in front of Tom, appearing so fragile in comparison with his bulk that he could have picked her up with one hand. Yet it was Tom who seemed, as her eyes sparked at him, on the verge of retreat.

"The pearls belong legally to the Lis, who are an honorable family. If Professor Li had not been murdered, if he had brought them here as he planned"—Lily spoke slowly and with meticulous enunciation—"they would have been declared at customs.

"As for the police, there are excellent reasons why we have not requested their help. First, the pearls have recently been brought out of Communist China. Madame Li has told me, and I believe her, that she does not think her husband was killed by communists. But the instant that word is mentioned, this situation will be turned into a political circus for crackpots and hysterics, for egomaniacs who want publicity, for local factions who are opposed to Hawaiian statehood. It will make newspaper headlines all over the country. And this will happen regardless of any actual facts which may be disclosed by police investigation.

"Madame Li will probably be a cripple for the rest of her life as a result of what was done to her. Such a physical indignity is something which she can endure so long as her personal privacy is not invaded. But to be stared at, followed by reporters and news photographers, pointed out by human ghouls every time she appears in public—*that* she would find intolerable.

"There is a second reason. No actual proof has been found that Yao was also murdered. If we ask the police to investigate, these people—Blanche Carleton, Hollis Knight, and whoever else is working with or directing them will immediately take cover. We would be unable to prevent them from leaving the islands. The pearls are small and easy to hide. Our hope is to find this criminal with them in his possession.

"We now come to the third reason, one which may have more weight with you. We know that any investigation must center around Paradise Teas. We do not wish to injure the reputation of a long-established and honorable business firm. Chinese have an expression: Do not break the other man's rice bowl. We need your help, but we do not wish to damage you in any way. If you should like me to explain further, to elaborate, perhaps—"

Tom held up a hand. "No, thanks. I might be slightly punchy at this point, but I can figure it out for myself." He smiled. "You can let your feathers down, Miss Wu. I apologize."

Lily looked up at him. The dimple in her cheek deepened. "My name," she said sweetly, "is Lily."

Tom wiped sweat from his forehead. "Whew!" Then he laughed. "It feels plenty warm in here. The tropics, I guess. Maybe we can cool off on the way to town. Shall we go?"

We parked some distance from the building and sauntered along the sidewalk, Lily's arm linked through Tom's on one side, mine on the other. Somewhere a record was playing shrill Oriental music. There was a smell of fresh-roasted coffee from the docks, and as we passed a darkened store the reek of soya and dried fish wafted to us on the hot night air.

"I keep reminding myself it's December," Tom said. "Probably snowing in New York now. What is that music—Chinese?"

"Japanese," Lily corrected.

Two figures walked past us, a slim young sailor in whites with a fat Portuguese girl on his arm. She wore orchids in her hair. They moved in an aura of rum. When we turned onto Maunakea Street they glanced back at us, then slowed their step. Shops were dark there, and empty.

Lily said quietly, "We will go up the alley."

We climbed rough wooden stairs to the loading platform. She handed a key to Tom. He said, "Flashlight, Janice?"

"I have it."

"You two girls wait just inside the door," he commanded. "I'll go ahead and reconnoiter."

I shoved the flashlight into his hand. The door swung open and we stepped into the pitch darkness of the warehouse. Tom's hand pressed my shoulder back and I stood there obediently beside Lily while he tiptoed across the floor, a beam of light preceding him. We watched the light go toward the packing room, then the warehouse seemed blacker as Tom put distance between us. He opened the door of the tasting room and stepped inside.

There was a thud. A grunting noise. Metal rattled on the floor and the light disappeared. I reached for Lily's hand. "Wait," she said into my ear.

We waited. I felt my hand begin to perspire in the clasp of hers. Then a small light shone in the tasting room. Someone let out a sharp little scream.

"Oh. Oh. Oh. Oh," she cried. "Oh. Oh. Oh."

We went to the sound.

The flashlight was on the floor, its beam turned to the bloody head of Tom Brittain. On her knees beside him, making those awful oh-oh noises, was Jean Hunter. She wasn't aware of us until we stood directly over her. Then she stared up into our faces.

"I've killed him!" she said, and went into a fit of appalling hysterics.

"Where's the light switch?" Lily asked. I felt the wall, knocked off a couple of tea canisters, and finally found it.

Lily bent over Tom while I pulled Jean away. There was a sink in the corner and I went to it and found a towel which I soaked with cold water and handed to Lily. She pressed it gently against Tom's head. When she lifted the towel, enough blood was blotted up to show a scalp wound about two inches long.

"It's a superficial cut," Lily said, and looked at Jean. "He isn't dead. Stop crying."

Jean gulped.

I soaked the towel again and Lily laid it on Tom's head. He moved and groaned.

At that sound Jean Hunter let out a little whimper of relief. She pushed Lily away and knelt by Tom. The first thing he saw when his eyes opened was her face bending over him.

"Oh, I am so sorry," she said, and tears spilled from her eyes and dropped on Tom's face.

He sat up and put a hand to his head. He looked at his bloody fingers, and then he looked at Jean. "You should be," he told her bitterly.

We were finally able to make some sense out of the situation. A look around the room explained part of it. There was a blanket on the floor where she had been lying. Near that was the gun she had used on Tom. Fortunately she hadn't enough nerve to fire, but had held it by the barrel and slugged him when he walked in the door. And after a while we got the truth.

Her uncle had lost his taste palate after he began to carouse with the Waikiki Widow. Jean tried to cover up for him. When tea arrived she locked them both into the room and did the tasting herself. She knew that Henry was short in his accounts but kept hoping that he would come to his senses and make up the loss—he could have borrowed on his insurance, she explained—before the Brittains discovered it.

She suspected that something was going on in the warehouse and had begun to sleep there whenever a new shipment arrived, trying to discover who was responsible. Thirty chests had just been delivered and she worked frantically to get it blended and packed before Tom started making inquiries and discovered that she was the taster.

"What kind of tea?" Some of Tom's bitterness seemed to be disappearing.

"Orange Pekoe. Uncle Henry wrote the formula for me once

when he was explaining the blending."

Tom smiled. "Did you get it all packaged?"

"Yes." Her voice was husky with tears. "The girls worked overtime."

"That's fine," he said and got to his feet. "I suppose this finishes us for tonight. We'd better get this girl home."

"While we're here," Lily said, "why don't we go upstairs?"

Jean went with us. She switched on the lights inside Hollis Knight's factory. She swayed against the wall and closed her eyes, and Tom guided her to a chair behind one of the sewing machines. Jean gave him a watery smile.

"She's exhausted," he explained superfluously. "No wonder, after the load she's been carrying." He patted her shoulder. "You stay there. We'll be through in a minute."

Hollis' office was walled on one side with shelves. Half of them contained boxes of jewelry, fans, ivory pieces, Oriental figures and enamelware. The rest held larger articles: bolts of silk, brocade squares, and pieces of embroidery and a few elaborate mandarin coats. The desk was locked, as was the steel filing cabinet and the small safe.

Tom was relieved to be finished. He and Jean started out of the building. Lily and I were following them when she halted and indicated a pile of matting in a corner of the room. "Is that from tea chests?"

Jean turned from the doorway. "Yes. Hollis is experimenting with table mats made from salvaged matting. Our boys brought this up a couple of weeks ago."

Tom and Jean went outside and sat on the steps. Lily hadn't move. She murmured, "A couple of weeks ago?" She went to the pile of mats. She began to pick up ragged and creased squares and toss them aside.

"What are you looking for?"

"I don't know," she told me. "I was just thinking—help me, Janice."

A few minutes later I lifted the last mat. Lily pointed to the floor. On the dusty, splintery wood there was a brown stain. As I tossed aside the mat I held, something rattled. Lily picked it up and turned, palm extended.

She was holding a broken denture, one of its incisors bright with a gold crown.

## CHAPTER SIXTEEN

"I'VE LOOKED EVERYWHERE," Jean Hunter said. "I don't know anything else to do."

We were back at our house on Tantalus. She sat on the *k'ang,* Tom by her side. Our blue silk cushions weren't kind to Jean's olive skin, her gray eyes were set in dark circles, and her mouth was pale. She was not, I thought pityingly, a very attractive girl.

Lily said, "Perhaps you have overlooked some small thing which might be a clue to where your uncle has gone. You must trust us—we want to help. Please tell us everything you can possibly remember."

We had not mentioned what we found under the straw mats. Jean was in no state to hear of that discovery.

She looked distressed at Lily's request. Tom leaned toward her. "Your face is dirty, kid." He brushed gently under her eyes with his handkerchief, and she blinked. Tom looked at his handkerchief, then back at Jean.

"It's her eyelashes," he said, "the shadow they make—"

Jean said, "Everything? Right from the beginning?"

"Yes."

She looked down at her lap and began: "I was in the office early that morning—"

"What morning?" Tom asked.

She hesitated. "I—right now I can't remember exactly."

"I sent some cables," Tom prompted.

She nodded. "It was the day your cable came. I called Uncle Henry at the house—he was sleeping late that morning—" Her hands flew apart. She clasped them again. "Where was I?"

Lily said, "Tom's cable . . ."

"Uncle Henry came to the office. He was worried. The Dragon Well—he hadn't bothered to—"

"It's unblended," Tom suggested. "Perhaps he didn't think it necessary to test it."

She gave him a grateful look. "He didn't even try. Your cable—Uncle Henry could have sent the second shipment out on an afternoon plane, but he didn't. He said it could go the next morning."

She looked at her hands again. "That night he went out, as usual—I thought, of course—there was no use asking questions."

Lily said, "He spent this evening—and many nights—with Lady Blanche, did he not?"

"Yes." She twined her fingers tighter. "I was upset because he hadn't sent the tea. I went to the movies. When I came home, Mr. Webster told me Uncle Henry had called. He wouldn't be in the next day. So I opened the office in the morning. The tea was stacked by the rear door, tagged for shipment. But one of the chests was soaked. There had been a leak during the night, from a lavatory upstairs. While I was trying to decide what to do, the pickup truck arrived, so I sent it off."

"Minus," Tom said, "the chest that was wet."

She nodded at him. "Uncle Henry didn't come home. When I didn't hear from him by the next afternoon, I began to worry. So I went to Waikiki. Lady Blanche's gate was locked."

"What did you do then?"

"I telephoned her house. The operator said the number had been temporarily disconnected. So I went out to Mokapuu."

"Where?" Tom asked.

"Mokapuu Point. Shortly after he met Lady Blanche my uncle leased a cottage from the Dawsons. Before he rented the Waikiki place for her they used to go there. The cottage was empty, so I came back to town and went to her house. I banged on the gate until a gardener finally answered. He said she had gone to the mainland."

"Then . . . ?" Lily prompted.

"I didn't know what to do. I was shocked to think Uncle Henry would leave the islands without a word to me. Finally I talked to Mr. Webster—"

"This guy Webster," Tom asked. "Who is he?"

"An old friend of my aunt's. He's a missionary, just arrived from China, staying at our house. I hated to bother him, he's not well—"

"But you decided to ask his advice?"

"Yes. I didn't want outsiders to know. He thought perhaps Uncle

Henry had quarreled with Lady Blanche and might have gone to one of the other islands." She gulped, "My uncle hasn't been himself."

"What happened next?" Lily asked.

Jean looked at Tom. "There was another cable. I didn't answer it. I kept hoping to hear from my uncle. When your transpacific call came, I told our housekeeper to say no one was home. I had just opened your message from the *Lurline* when Hollis came in and said that Lady Blanche was arriving. I was confused. I thought maybe the three of you were traveling together, then I decided that didn't make sense. All I could do was wait until the ship arrived—"

"I saw you at the dock," I told her.

"I didn't see you. I missed Lady Blanche too. When I telephoned, her houseboy said she wouldn't be home until later. Mr. Webster offered to go and see her that afternoon. I was so busy, trying to get the tea packed before you came in and found out—" Her voice broke and she began to shiver.

"She's had enough," Tom growled. "I'm going to take her home."

"We'll drive you," Lily said.

When he came back from Jean's door and got into the car, I started toward Nuuanu. Tom said, "Is this the way to the beach?"

"No," Lily told him. "We re going to Mokapuu Point." She reported what we had found in Hollis Knight's factory.

"Jean did not see her uncle after the second shipment of Dragon Well arrived. When he went out that evening she thought he was going, as usual, to see Lady Blanche. But we know that Blanche was by then in San Francisco."

"I get it," Tom said. "Hunter went back just like we did tonight, to find out who was meddling with the tea."

"Yes," Lily said. "It is significant, I think, that he did not send it on to New York immediately, in spite of your cable."

"You think he was attacked in the building?"

"It is possible. He might have lain under the mats for a while, until arrangements could be made to take him somewhere else." She added thoughtfully, "The police are equipped for searching. If we discover nothing at Mokapuu, we must notify them."

"That'll be a relief," Tom said. "Do you know how to find this place, Janice?"

"I know where the Dawson cottage is. I was there once. But I hope you've still got that flashlight."

"It's here."

We hardly needed it by the time we reached the cottage. The narrow, rutted road ended at a hill. From there a footpath led over the rise and down to the cove where the little house stood. No other house was near and the place was hidden from view unless approached by water. The eastern sky was paling as we trudged down the path. A gunmetal sea sent little waves shoreward to leave scallops of froth on the sand.

Seaward windows were shuttered against salt spray and the entrance was protected by a wooden storm door tied from inside. Tom said, "Got any tools in the car?"

"In the luggage compartment."

He used a screwdriver to force the latch which held the rear door. He stepped inside, then stopped so short that my nose bumped his spine. He backed slowly, closing the door. "You girls better stay here. I'll go in alone."

We looked at him. He muttered, "I was in the war. I know what that smell means."

I had never encountered it before, but I knew it too. Even outside, with morning breeze fresh against our faces, that stench seemed to linger.

When Tom came out he said, "You can go in now. If you want to."

Lily asked, "Is it Henry Hunter?"

"I think so. I found him in the pantry. The side of his head is crushed."

She said, "I will go in."

I followed her, holding a handkerchief over my nose. At the door of the pantry I stopped, my eyes drawn to a faded lavender bedspread flung over something on the floor. I saw one shoe, one ankle covered by a silk sock with a jaunty green arrow embroidered on it.

Then I fled and leaned against a rock, stomach heaving, until they came out.

## CHAPTER SEVENTEEN

WE SLEPT FOR A few hours after we returned to Honolulu, Lily and I in our beds and Tom in the living room with feet hanging off the end of the *k'ang*. I had left a note for Shizu to awaken us when she came in, and I opened my eyes to find her standing by the bed with a cup of coffee.

"How about Mr. Brittain?"

"He's awake," she said. "Waiting in the garden."

After breakfast Lily asked Tom, "Are you going to the office now?"

He looked at his wrinkled trousers. "After I change."

"How about you, Janice?" Which meant that Lily had plans of her own.

"It might help Tom if I tagged along to the office."

He liked the idea. "I'll call Jean Hunter and tell her to stay home today. She's probably worn out."

Both Lily and I had enjoyed less than four hours sleep—but then, neither of us had eyelashes half an inch long. And I had pitied Jean for being so unattractive. *Men!* I thought, again. They're wonderful. As soon as you're sure you know them they come up with something like this.

I waited in the car until Tom returned from his hotel room dressed in white linen, his hair dampened and brushed flat, his face smelling of aftershave lotion. As I pressed the starter he said, "Before we go to the office, Janice, I want to see Blanche."

"Blanche? What for?"

"I've got an idea that she might tell us what we want to know. If she's handled right."

And obviously he thought he was the man to do it. Maybe he was, at that. Blanche was a man's woman. And this man . . . I sent him a sharp glance. Today he didn't look fatuous or happy or smug. He looked determined.

As we drove along Kalakaua toward Blanche's house, I said suddenly, "Tom. We know each other pretty well by now, don't we?"

"Sure," he said. "What are you working up to?"

"I want to ask you a question."

"Shoot."

"Have you and Blanche—I mean, did you—are you—"

"If you want to know whether I got between the sheets with her, the answer is no. Postscript: I don't want to."

"Then what makes you think you can persuade her to talk?"

"I've got a bribe to offer. That's the language Blanche understands."

I said, surprised, "You sound as if you don't even like her."

"No, Janice. I never did. But I knew one of you was playing games. Until I found out which, I had to go along."

"But Blanche," I said, "she's really fascinating, she has a lot of sex appeal and—"

"—and a whore's mentality," he finished. "I don't like whores, Janice."

*Well!*

"There's another thing," he said, "which you don't seem to realize. Blanche's type is passé. Oh, she might go over with some poor sex-starved guy like Hunter or a bullish type like Dan Gordon, especially in a tropical atmosphere or in the Orient where there's an acute shortage of blondes. There isn't any shortage in America."

I remembered then that Blanche's husband had been many years her senior. I said with new respect in my voice, "What are you going to say to her?"

He told me, the rest of the way to her house. When we stopped there we found the bamboo gate locked.

"Her houseboy probably doesn't come until noon," I suggested.

"We won't wait for him," Tom said. "Drive up alongside the fence."

When I did so he climbed to the top of the car and jumped into Blanche's garden, then opened the gates while I drove in. The place was utterly quiet. The swimming pool mirrored the sky like blue glass. Doors to the living room were shut. When we slid one back, cold air came out at us. We went through to the hall to Blanche's bedroom.

At Tom's knock a sleepy voice asked, "Who's there?"

"It's Tom."

"Tom? What time is it, for heaven's—" The words were lost in a yawn. "Tom?" A soft laugh. "You must be completely mad, darling."

The door opened. Blanche stood there in sheer pink nylon, raising white arms over her head, smiling—until she saw me. Her smile vanished, she retreated a step, then said, "You've got a nerve! How did you get in here?"

Tom said, "Take it easy, lovely. We want to talk to you."

She went to a chair for a negligee, turning her back as she slipped her arms into it. She said over her shoulder, her voice cautious now, "What do you want?"

Tom said, "I've got a little proposition for you. May we sit down?"

Blanche watched us, moving backward to her bed. When her legs touched it she sat. Tom took a chair and I settled on the satin chaise.

He began, "We found Henry Hunter's body last night."

"Henry's body?" She wet her lips.

"The police haven't been notified yet," Tom said. "I wanted to give you a sporting chance before we report his murder."

"Murder? I know nothing about it." She crossed one leg over the other. "I was on the mainland at the—" Then she looked at Tom with wide blue eyes. Tom might call her passé, I thought, but she was damned attractive, even with her hair disarranged, and then I observed that she was wearing makeup. What for? Or, rather, for whom? Gordon was on his way to Manila, Tom had been with us, Henry was dead. Hollis Knight? Or someone else? I looked at the two pillows on her bed. Both were mussed. That didn't mean anything, really.

Tom had let silence grow in the room. Then he said, "How did you know, Blanche, when Hunter was killed?"

She dropped a pink mule from one foot, then concentrated on getting her toes into it again. "I didn't. I have been in California, remember?"

I made my contribution. "Let's quit horsing around, Blanche. You know something we want to find out. Tom is offering you a chance now to give us that information—in exchange for your life."

Blanche stared at me. She said furiously, "What do you mean, in exchange for my life? Of all the bloody nonsense!"

I looked straight back at her. "You're liable to be indicted as accessory to the murder of Henry Hunter. No, wait a minute. His body was found in the beach cottage where he used to take you.

Certain personal possessions of yours are still there—"

"Like hell they are!" she said. "There isn't a single thing that wasn't—" She stopped. She pulled pink satin tight across her stomach as if she felt, suddenly, without adequate protection.

"Blanche," I said, "*you* may have taken away everything you left there. But *someone* has put things back. Have you missed any lingerie, stockings, or certain, er, other intimate feminine articles?"

Her blue eyes glazed. She was trying to remember. I added, "And of course, your fingerprints are all over the place."

"What if I was there?" Her foot began to swing. "That doesn't mean murder."

While I talked, Tom had risen and gone to look at the aquarium where angelfish floated in the lighted bubbling water. He turned and said to her, "It might not mean murder, lovely. But it does mean investigation. I can testify that Hunter embezzled from my firm in order to pay your rent, to buy the clothes you wear. And when you had milked him dry, you made a play for me.

"All this adds up to a picture that isn't very pretty. You're in the United States now. And as you probably know, this has become an extremely moral country recently. The State Department has never been so interested in the private lives of aliens. Especially those suspected of what we Americans quaintly call 'moral turpitude.'"

The foot stopped swinging. She sat straight. "I am the wife of a British diplomat."

"You are his widow," Tom corrected. "There's a world of difference."

"And what's more," I put in, "you haven't any money. Your husband signed over everything to his sister. We know all about the poor but haughty Carletons. We also know quite a lot about the kind of background you left when you went out to Singapore as a nurse. I'm very sure that you don't want to go back to England."

Blanche stared at me almost with fear. The fact that we had found out so much about her seemed a terrific shock. Tom sent me a surprised glance. At his side, where Blanche couldn't see the gesture, his fingers made the O which signifies approval.

I went on, "You'll be interested to know that your husband's sister is having difficulty keeping up that huge old place without a domestic staff. Recently she advertised for someone to help with the dog kennels—it's Sealyhams, isn't it? She might be glad to have you at that, in exchange for your services."

Blanche jerked to her feet. "All right, you goddamned sanctimonious bitch! I don't want to go back. And what is more, I don't intend to."

Tom observed, "You won't be permitted to stay here. British Hong Kong won't want you—you have no income."

She stood, in the middle of the carpeted floor, her shoulders drooping, and she looked for a moment quite pitiful, very feminine and defenseless. Tom moved to her side and put an arm around her for a moment and she swayed toward him. He said in a softer voice, "Look, lovely. You're a gambler. I'm going to offer you a gambling proposition. Tell us who your pals are, and I'll help you."

This time she didn't pretend to misunderstand. She said in a low voice, "You'll help me to what?"

"To a safe future. Here's the deal. I'm opening a restaurant in New York soon. It will cater to a cosmopolitan clientele. I need a hostess, someone like you who is beautiful, charming, soigneé. The job will pay a good salary, enough for you to live and dress well. And you'll meet men by the score."

She said, "And what if this proposition doesn't appeal to me?"

Tom shrugged. "It's your decision. You might like it better than cleaning dog kennels. Or, at the very least, being deported as an undesirable alien."

It seemed to me that he was almost pleading. I felt annoyed. I stood up and said, "No matter what happens, Blanche, you aren't going to front for anybody from now on. You'll be watched wherever you go. This will make you a handicap and a danger—"

Blanche's hand went to her mouth. Her face grew pinched and she suddenly looked old. That was the shot which scored.

She turned to Tom and said, "Can I speak with you alone?"

I started to protest. "I don't see why—" but Tom said, "Why not? Scram, Janice. I'll meet you outside."

I went reluctantly. I walked up and down the lanai for perhaps five minutes, until Tom came out. I said, "What . . . ?" and Tom told me, "She wants a little time to think things over."

"But that's ridiculous! She'll warn—"

"What if she does? As you've said, this is an island, nobody can get away from here. And you're watching her. No matter what she does, we can't lose."

But I still felt disturbed. I was sure we were making a mistake, and I told him so. Tom said stubbornly, "I told her she could have until five o'clock. If you think you can force things by going back and arguing with the woman, go right ahead. Otherwise we're to come back here at five."

We headed toward Kalakaua Avenue. It was a wonderful day. Little cottony clouds fluffed along the sky, coca palms swished playfully in the trades, there was a good surf combing the reef and already people were sprawled over the yellow sands or splashing in the water. Tom looked at the scene and sighed.

"It's work today for me. We'd better get to the office."

I turned to the curbing and stopped. "I've changed my mind about going downtown. Maybe I'll be there later. You can get a taxi or take the trolley bus here."

He said, his hand on the door, "You're sore, aren't you?"

"Not exactly. I'm worried. And I just thought of something else I want to do right now."

As soon as he was out of sight, I went into a drugstore and called our house. Shizu said Lily wasn't there. She had gone to see somebody named Tseng. No, she didn't know the address. I hung up with a feeling of frustration. Then I drove back to Blanche's house. A hundred feet or so from the bamboo gates I had seen a parked car. I slowed beside it and said to the Chinese girl who sat with a book propped before her on the steering wheel, "Is your name Tseng?"

"Yes," she said. "I'm Iris. You're Janice Cameron, aren't you?"

I nodded. "My friend Lily has gone to your house. Where are you staying?"

She told me and I thanked her and started toward Manoa Valley.

Mr. Hartford Tseng met me at the door of the big stone house which was his temporary domicile on Oahu. "Welcome," he said. "Come inside and meet my children."

I followed him to a lanai which spread along the side of the house, where the flagged floor was covered with woven straw matting fine as silk, chairs and swings and couches were piled with pillows, there were books and magazines and boxes of candy and radios and a record player and a ping-pong table with two embroidered satin slippers under it and a chessboard scattered with pieces and an easel with a canvas on it and a portable typewriter—everything in profusion and confusion.

There were two Chinese girls there, one of whom I recognized. She jumped to her feet as we appeared. "Hello," she said. "Remember me? I'm Orchid Tseng."

"Hello, Orchid. Where's Lily Wu?"

"Here," she said from the depths of a big rattan chair.

Mr. Tseng lowered himself to a *punee*. He waved a hand. "And this incredibly hideous creature," he said with a chuckle, "is my other daughter, Verbena. The girls will now leave us."

They rose and bowed. Dimples showed, black eyes sparkled as they bowed again toward their father and then ran from the lanai. We could hear them giggling inside the house..

I looked at Mr. Tseng. "You have my profound sympathy, sir," I said with a straight face, "that the gods have chosen to afflict you with such ill-favored children."

His mouth opened. Then he roared and slapped a hand on his fat, silk-covered knees.

"Delightful!" he said, "Except for your unfortunate coloring, Miss Cameron, and a few other, er—minor details, you might be Chinese."

He clapped his hands. Instantly a servant appeared, nodded at Tseng's rapid orders, and withdrew. A few minutes later we were drinking hot fragrant tea and nibbling sesame cakes.

Our host said, "You two have something to tell me. What has happened?"

Lily told him. After her first words his face grew blank. He fixed bright black eyes on her and sat utterly still while he listened.

"So," he said softly, when she finished, "another man has died for Tz'u Hsi's pearls. Have you reported the discovery of Mr. Hunter's body?"

"Not yet," Lily said. "He has been there for several days already. A little while longer can make no difference. The third shipment of

Dragon Well should be due soon, and when that arrives, we may trap the murderer."

"Lily," I said, "you're counting on the fact that our interest is unsuspected. That's not the case any more."

She said sharply, "What do you mean?"

"I mean that Tom Brittain has spilled the beans." I told them about our visit to Blanche Carleton.

Mr. Tseng asked, "And what will he do with this woman if she decides not to betray her associates?"

"I don't know," I said uneasily. "When we were on our way to her house, he talked in a very lofty tone about how he detested women of her type. But I noticed that as soon as he was near her for a while his attitude changed. I think we made a serious mistake."

"You can't alter the situation by worrying," Lily told me. "But I agree with you that we should not wait until five o'clock. Before we go, however, I want to ask Mr. Tseng something."

She turned to him and said, "When Yao was dying he wrote two characters for me. Dragon was one. We know now that he meant Tea of the Well of the Dragon. The other character was Tiger. Tom Brittain says there is no Tiger tea of any kind. Can you think of anything in connection with this word?"

Tseng stroked his bald head and looked thoughtful. "There are Tiger hats which little boys wear."

"And Tiger Whiskers," Lily contributed, "are used by some herbalists."

Which makes me think," he said, "of Tiger Balm. The man who concocted it made a fortune."

"I've heard of that," I said. "Tiger Balm was supposed to cure anything, even astigmatism."

Lily's fine brows drew together slightly. "Astigmatism," she said, "it reminds me—"

Tseng exclaimed, "Tiger Eyes! That's what many peasants call Caucasians in China. They are afraid of light-eyed people."

"Madame Li said to me once," I recalled, "that at least I did not have light eyes. I wondered what she meant."

Lily rose from the chair and began to pace the floor. "What color are Hollis Knight's eyes?"

"They're brown."

"Blanche Carleton has blue eyes. But she was with us at the time Yao was killed. The only other person who has arrived recently from China is the missionary, Matthew Webster. I've never spoken to him, Janice, but you have. Are his eyes blue?"

"No-o-o," I said. "They're a sort of pale hazel, almost amber . . ."

We looked at each other.

I said, "He told me, the first night he was here, that his mission in Ningpo had been burned."

Lily said, "Yao came from Ningpo."

She spoke to Tseng. "Is there any way to check with the Presbyterian Mission Board?"

"Our family attends the Presbyterian Church. I will ask the pastor."

We went home then, to bathe and get some rest. When we reached the house, I called Steve Dugan at the newspaper office.

"Steve, can you do a little more checking for us?"

"Sure. What do you want?"

"The passenger list of the American President Lines, the last two ships in port. See if a Matthew Webster was on it, and if he traveled alone."

"Okay. I'll call you back."

As we waited for Steve's call I said, "Tell me about the Tseng family. How does Mr. Hartford Tseng happen to have seven daughters?"

"Because," Lily said, "he loves children."

"Then why has he never married?"

"He is a eunuch."

I gasped. I tried to say something, but could not.

Lily said, "He was a slave of the Dowager Empress, as I told you. There were more than four thousand eunuch slaves in the forbidden City during the time of Tz'u Hsi. He was one of the few who escaped. Just before the last war he sold his holdings in Java and came to America. Over a period of years he adopted deserted and orphaned children until he now has this family."

"And he wants to buy some of the pearls because of what they mean to him, as symbols of his freedom. Is that it?"

Lily smiled. "That is as good a reason as any."

The telephone rang and I answered it. Steve said, "I checked American President for you, sweetie. The guy was never on it. He arrived by Hong Kong clipper on the eighth of November."

"Thanks, Steve."

"Janice," she said, "you gonna have a nice story for me pretty soon?"

"It isn't very nice, Steve. But we'll let you know the minute we can."

"It's a deal. So long."

"The eighth of November," Lily repeated, "And Henry Hunter met him at the President dock three weeks later. Why do you suppose Mr. Hunter lied?"

"Maybe he didn't. Webster could have pretended to arrive—that's easy enough to do. There's always a lot of confusion at a ship's arrival." I added slowly, "But he's a missionary, Lily. It doesn't make sense."

"It doesn't seem to," she admitted. "But perhaps that is because we don't have all the facts. Mr. Tseng's Presbyterian pastor may be able to add a few. In the meantime I am going to take a shower."

"I suppose I should go to Tom's office," I said. "But I don't want to go. I'm too jittery."

That feeling didn't leave me. It persisted, and grew so strong that I couldn't finish lunch. I pushed back my plate and lit a cigarette and finally recognized my jitters as a sense of calamity.

"Lily," I said. "I don't think we should wait any longer. We ought to go to Waikiki now."

She rose from the table. "All right. But in fairness to him we must tell Tom Brittain."

When I called Tom, an indifferent voice, which I recognized as that of the blonde in the outer reception room, said that he wasn't in. No, she didn't know where he had gone. No, she didn't know when he would return. I left my name and a message that I had called and would call again later and she said yeah she would tell him. I repeated this to Lily and said again that I thought we should not wait and she said all right and then we got into the car and started to the beach to see Blanche Carleton.

## CHAPTER EIGHTEEN

THE AFTERNOON SUN WAS HOT on the graveled drive of Blanche's house. The bamboo gates stood open. When we parked the car we saw a delivery truck at the rear service entrance. Its open doors revealed baskets of groceries. We walked around to the lanai and looked into the empty living room. Somewhere inside the house a vacuum cleaner began to snarl.

"The houseboy can't hear us," I said, and slid a glass panel into the wall. The vacuum cleaner sounded louder then.

We waited in the living room and, when no one appeared, walked to the passage which bisected the house. The boy seemed to be cleaning the room next to Blanche's. I knocked and, when she did not answer, called, "Blanche?" and opened the door.

The room was a shambles: clothes tossed to the floor, contents of drawers dumped everywhere, the satin-upholstered mattress ripped and gouged. Even the aquarium had been knocked sideways and most of the water splashed out. The silly little diver lay half submerged and air bubbled out of his helmet as if he were gargling. The French door to the garden stood open and sheer curtains rippled in a faint breeze. The vacuum cleaner still whined in the next room, but above its noise we heard a car back and turn and race along the drive.

We got to the lanai in time to see the grocery truck disappear through the bamboo gates, its rear doors flapping. In the room next to Blanche's we found the vacuum cleaner standing in the middle of the floor with its motor running. I turned it off, and the quiet was almost startling.

We went next door again, to the bathroom. We found Blanche there, her arms raised, swaying against the steel-framed shower door. She wore what was left of a white tricot slip. Her wrists were tied with a nylon stocking and she was held upright by a pair of nylons knotted together and looped over the frame. There was a burnt smell. It came from Blanche's back, where a wad of cotton, stuck to her flesh by adhesive tape, was smoldering. On the rim of the bathtub was a can of lighter fluid.

Lily yanked the cotton from Blanche's back while I reached for the stocking. At my touch Blanche's head lifted, she said thickly, "No! No!"

"It's only Janice," I said. "I'm trying to get you down. Stand up for a minute if you can, while I pull this thing off."

When I slipped the stocking over the door-frame Blanche sank to her knees, and I braced her jerking body while she leaned over the tub and retched. After a while I turned the tap and she cupped her hands and held cold water to her face, gasping. Lily opened the door of the medicine cabinet and asked quietly, "Do you have any kind of burn ointment?"

Blanche shook her head. Lily found some cold cream and laid a blob of it on Blanche's back. We got her into the other room and onto the ruined mattress, where she lay shuddering and breathing harshly. When Lily came back from the bar with a glass of whiskey Blanche spilled half while I dried her face with my handkerchief.

We lit cigarettes and sat down. When Blanche finally stopped shivering, Lily said, "It is a good thing that we did not wait until five o'clock."

Blanche said, "Could I have another drink?"

She took it without spilling and accepted the cigarette I gave her. Lily disentangled pillows from bedding on the floor and put them behind Blanche's head. She sat propped, smoking and looking around the room, dully at first and then with dismay as she became aware of the wreckage. Her concern finally focused on the aquarium, beneath which something moved. A fish, flopping on the soaked carpet. She jumped from the bed and picked it up and dropped it into the tank. She grabbed a big crystal vase of yellow ginger which had somehow escaped being broken and dumped water and flowers into the tank. The effort seemed to exhaust her and she staggered to the bed and sat with her head drooping, breathing fast. Shock, I thought. People do ridiculous things sometimes.

Lily said, "What did he want, Blanche?"

"Want?" Blanche seemed oh the verge of fainting. She closed her eyes and flopped back.

Lily said, again, "What did he want? Was it the pearls?"

The woman on the bed did not answer.

Lily said, "If we had arrived later, we might have found you dead."

No response.

Lily took a hand mirror from a jumble of cosmetics on the dressing table and held it before Blanche, saying, "Would you like to look at your face?"

Blanche sat up. She snatched the mirror from Lily and stared into it. She raised shaking fingers to her bruised mouth, to an ugly purple mark at her temple. She dropped the mirror and looked around the room again, then pointed to a straw purse which lay by the closet door. "Bring it to me," she said.

When I brought it she dumped the contents on the bed: compact, lipstick and brush, perfume flacon, and a large flat wallet. She snatched this and opened it, then sagged with relief as she found her passport.

She said then, her voice flat with hatred, "His name isn't Webster."

Both Lily and I leaned forward. She said, "What is his name?"

"Joe Donnelly. I met him in Shanghai in 1948. He's been in China for years, he speaks Chinese. He came out originally to join Chennault's A.V.G. group. Later he was commissioned in the Air Force."

"British?" Lily asked.

"American. When I met him he was in uniform; he had plenty of money. Everybody was crazy about fliers then. My husband was in London . . ."

I had heard about those years in China, when Chennault's fliers were idolized by the people. With her elderly husband absent, in a city infamous for its gaudy, frenzied night life, its atmosphere tense with war nerves, a woman like Blanche must have let the bars down completely.

She said, "When Simon returned, we were transferred from Shanghai. I thought I would never see Joe again. But three months ago he showed up at our house in Hong Kong. He said he had just gotten out of China. He'd stayed there after the communists came, as a flying instructor. He looked terrible, at least twenty years older. He is sick—"

"What's wrong with him?" I asked.

"*Kali azar.*"

At my puzzled look Lily said, "It is a parasitical disease rather common in China. The symptoms are similar to malaria but *kali azar* is generally fatal. They are experimenting now with—" She looked at Blanche. "He wanted to come to America for treatment?"

"Yes. He had no money. But he had got some pearls from a missionary he knew in Ningpo. The man had died and Joe was traveling on his papers. He offered me half the pearls if I would take them through customs for him."

I was beginning to understand. "And, as Sir Simon Carleton's wife, you had diplomatic immunity."

"Yes. But Simon died just before we were due to sail. He left no money, and I hadn't any choice but to go back to England. Joe said that if I would help him get the pearls to the States we would be married and, as the wife of an American, I could stay. He had found out from the missionary's letters that he was a friend of Mrs. Hunter's. She suggested once that if Mr. Webster ever went to Hong Kong he should look up Hollis Knight, and she gave his office address."

"I wondered how you happened to know him," I said.

"I met Hollis with the pretext of selling my husband's jade collection. After—later on I sounded him out on the possibility of sending the pearls through in one of his shipments. He refused to take the risk. But he came around later and suggested using the tea firm. He could get Dragon Well tea on the black market and thought if he offered it cheaply enough Henry would buy it.

"There were ninety-nine pearls. We divided them into three lots, one for each of us. Hollis got the tea and they packed the chests and he left them in his godown for a clerk to forward in three separate shipments. Then Joe suggested I had better get acquainted with Henry in order to keep a check on Hollis. I came here and met Henry—" She looked at me. "Is he really dead?"

"Yes."

"I had nothing to do with that."

"We believe you," Lily assured her. "What about this man named Joe?"

"He came over soon after I did, on the clipper. He took a room in a cheap hotel and I helped him change his hair—it was gray, but Webster had white hair, so we dyed his white. He found a doctor down on River Street to give him some shots for his fever while we experimented with the hair dye. Then he had Hollis' clerk send a cable announcing his arrival on a President ship. By that time the first lot had arrived and they opened it and took out the pearls. We did not expect Tom Brittain to order the tea sent on to New York. That caused trouble, but they managed to get the second chest. You say Henry is dead. He must have caught them at it."

Lily said, "And you have been keeping the pearls?"

Blanche sent her a small, derisive smile. "Joe wouldn't trust anybody. This morning the Hunter girl told him about what happened in the building last night. He knows I've been seeing you both. He came here and accused me of planning to double-cross him."

Lily went to the bed. She said, looking steadily down at Blanche, "He was searching this room. He tortured you. What does he want?"

Blanche opened the wallet and took a folded piece of yellow paper from the money section. "He wants this," she said. "I took it from him once, a long time ago, when he was drunk. It is very important to him."

I went to Lily's side to read it and saw a sales slip from a Waikiki beauty salon indicating that Blanche had paid three dollars for two ounces of individually blended face powder.

She explained, "When I ordered it I left my own powder box to put it in. The box had a false bottom. Under it you will find an Air Force identification tag for Joseph Donnelly." Her laugh was short and harsh. "I hope he hangs."

Lily put the paper in her purse. "Janice," she said, "we had better go now."

Blanche jerked erect. "What's going to happen to me?"

Lily didn't answer that. She asked, instead, "Was it you who called Yao at the clinic?"

"I don't know what you're talking about." Her bewilderment seemed genuine.

"It was a woman who asked for Yao. If it wasn't you, who was it?"

"Some waitress."

I said, feeling sorry for her, "Blanche, if you had nothing to do with Henry's death—we'll see that you get a good lawyer. And after it's all over maybe you can take that job with Tom. New York's a wonderful place—you might like living there."

She looked down and her fingers tightened around the passport. "I might," she said. Then she stood up. "But I can't stay here alone. And I can't waste money on a hotel. Wait, will you, while I make a phone call."

I followed her to the library where she called the Moana and asked for Mrs. Harry Fentriss. "Dorothy?" she said sweetly, "Why don't you and Harry come over this afternoon? I'd love to see you."

There was excited chatter over the wire.

"Good!" Blanche said. "Bring them along. This is my boy's day off, but we can serve ourselves. And there's plenty of everything left from last night. Bring suits, if you want to swim. Some more friends may drop over later. We'll have an impromptu party."

She cradled the telephone and, as we went back to her room, said, "Please stay until they come."

I said we would stay.

While we waited, Blanche peeled the torn slip over her head. She stood naked before the mirror and turned sideways to examine herself. She brought a bandage and a piece of cotton from the bathroom and said, "Stick this on for me, will you?"

I fastened it over the raw red circle between her shoulder blades and found that she was more steady than I. Perhaps it didn't hurt yet. Perhaps by betraying the man who had done this to her she had anesthetized herself.

She rummaged through lingerie on the floor and found a lace bra and garter belt and stockings which she put on; she examined bottles and jars with a brief nod of satisfaction as she found them unbroken. She leaned forward to study her face intently as she smoothed foundation lotion, liquid powder, and eye shadow with quick, expert strokes.

Lily, who cannot tolerate untidiness, had begun to pick up bureau drawers and slide them back into place, and I followed her example, unable to resist glancing frequently at Blanche as she concentrated on the mirror. Such a detached attitude fascinated me. Blanche regarded her physical self, apparently, as an instrument. Yet while she applied makeup I had the impression that these gestures were automatic and her mind was furiously busy on something completely apart from what she was doing.

Lily tucked sheets around the ruined mattress and smoothed the spread. She too was withdrawn and her movements were as automatic as those of Blanche. She went to the aquarium and began to pick out stalks of ginger, and Blanche, who was tilted over the hand mirror with mascara brush in her hand, said, "Would you put some water in the tanks? I promised the agent I would take care of those fish."

Lily filled the crystal vase with water from the tub and made several trips to the tank. One angelfish was half floating and I said, "That one will probably die. They're delicate."

Blanche shrugged. "I'll get another one."

She laid down her lipstick brush and stood up, apparently satisfied. Her eyes were bright. Except for a slight swelling around her mouth and the bruise at her temple, she looked much the same as usual. She said, "I have a strapless shantung with a bolero which will cover the bandage."

As she zipped herself into it I regarded her with half admiration, half incredulity. The furious concentration had been on what she was to wear. I looked at Lily to see whether she registered this, but Lily was still deep in whatever she had been pondering. Now she said, "I think I'll go to the shop and get that face powder. I should be back by the time Blanche's guests arrive."

Blanche hesitated, then slipped her arms into the jacket of her dress. "I don't think he'll come back now. He stole that grocery truck in order to get in here. Are you going to have him arrested?"

"I have been trying to think of what is best to do," Lily told her. "Perhaps we should wait until the third shipment is here." At the door she stopped. "If we can catch both men in the act of opening the tea chest, perhaps you won't have to testify."

Blanche nodded, apparently satisfied.

Just after Lily left, the Fentrisses arrived with a Mr. and Mrs. Atkins from Evansville, whom they had met at the hotel. Dorothy Fentriss was wearing a bright Polynesian print and barefoot sandal. Mrs. Atkins, plump and full-bosomed, was in white sharkskin. Both women wore leis and Dorothy had brought a wreath of vanda orchids for Blanche. She was thrilled at being here. She enjoyed saying, "This is our dear friend, Lady Blanche Carleton."

The Atkinses were in that state of euphoria common to tourists, heightened now by meeting a cosmopolitan beauty with a title. Blanche was vivacious, animated with that feverishness I had observed the first night we met. She accepted the orchid lei and Dorothy's kiss with a brilliant smile and said it was charming of her, she was delighted to see them all.

She switched on the radio and music sounded through a speaker on the lanai. I went to the bar to watch Harry Fentriss mix drinks. He was sunburned, he wore a silk shirt patterned with red and orange fish and he liked being bartender. When Dorothy came over to us he said, admiring the zebra-skin bar, "Wouldn't it slay 'em at home, honey, if we got ourselves something like this? How about having our rumpus room done over when we get back?"

"I don't care if we never get back;" Dorothy declared, and added in a wail, "It just kills me to think of leaving here, and we've only got four days more!"

Her husband shoved a glass at her. "Take this and quit bawling," he said. "Let's enjoy those four days while we can." His eyes widened and he exclaimed, "My God! Look who's coming!"

We turned and saw Lily Wu getting out of the car. A yellow Cadillac pulled up alongside the Plymouth and Gogo Leung, smooth in white linen, came around and opened the door for Betty Chang. The three Chinese walked toward Blanche and I heard Gogo say, "We hear by coconut wireless that a party's in the making."

Blanche greeted them, made introductions, and brought them to the bar to meet Harry and Dorothy. The Atkinses exchanged beatific glances which said that this was going to be something to tell Evansville about—and the day was only beginning!

Lily carried a small package. She signaled Blanche with raised brows. "I'd like to freshen up a bit, if I may."

"Of course," Blanche said. "I'll show you the way."

We went back to Blanche's bedroom and Lily handed her the package. Blanche unwrapped a square satin box and dumped the powder it contained onto the wrapping paper. She pried up the bottom with a nail file and took out a rectangular metal identification disc, blew powder from it and gave it to Lily. Stamped into the metal was the name, "Joseph P. Donnelly," then there were some numbers and the letters A and C.

Lily said, touching them, "Blood type and religion, I suppose." She put the disc in her purse and said to Blanche, "I brought Gogo and Betty because it seemed safer for you to have a crowd here. Perhaps, if you have some kind of party and it lasts long enough—"

Blanche said, "That is what I have been thinking. I might persuade the Fentrisses to stay overnight." She looked at me. "Do you think those actors might like to come?"

"Some of them have left by now. I think Alan and the camera crew are on Kauai. I can call them if you like."

Lily said from the dressing table, "While you're telephoning I'll fix my face."

Blanche returned to her guests while I went to the telephone in the library. Alan wasn't at the hotel but I left a message. It was almost four by then and I called Tom Brittain. "Tom," I said, "we're at Waikiki and—"

"Want to come to the office?" he said guardedly. "I just came from the tea examiner. The Dragon Well is here. I'm waiting for the truck to arrive now."

## CHAPTER NINETEEN

WHEN WE REACHED Paradise Teas, Tom met us in the reception room. He was annoyed. "I didn't mind your not coming here, Janice," he said. "But why didn't you call me?"

It was ten minutes of four and the ratty blonde was slinging the cover over her typewriter. I said, "Tom, I did call. This girl took the message."

He scowled at her. "Why didn't you tell me?"

She stared back insolently. "I forgot."

Tom started to speak, then waited as if counting to ten. He said, "When you leave tonight, take everything you own from that desk. You're fired!"

For a moment she was frightened, then she leaned back in her chair and sneered. "You can't fire me. You're not my boss."

Tom's hands clenched at his sides. "*I am firing you now*. My firms pay part of your salary. I won't have such a slovenly employee around this place."

Her eyes behind stiff, mascaraed lashes grew hard. "We'll see about that." She pushed a key on the intercom. "Mr. Knight, can you come down a minute?"

There was a squawk.

"I know you are, Mr. Knight. But this is an emergency."

When Hollis appeared she whined, "Mr. Brittain is trying to fire me. I told him I work for you but he—"

Hollis looked at Tom. "What's the matter?"'

Tom said tersely, "She's slovenly and inefficient. Today she failed to give me an important message. I don't want her around here."

Hollis' face grew red. He said, "Perhaps we'd better discuss it later."

He turned to the girl with a conciliatory smile. "You'd better run up to my office. I'm busy right now, but we'll try to straighten this out."

The blonde switched out of the room. Hollis looked at Tom, started to speak, shrugged, and followed her. We three went into Tom's office.

Lily said, "Tell us about the tea."

Tom sat at his desk and began. "I went over to the tea examiner's today, just to identify myself and tell them my manager is away for a while." He frowned. "We shouldn't leave Hunter out there much longer."

"We won't," Lily said. "Please continue."

"Well, I introduced myself and asked casually whether any shipments were due to arrive. They looked surprised and said of course a shipment had arrived. They mailed the notice yesterday."

"And it was Dragon Well?"

"It must be. We haven't anything else coming from Hong Kong."

There were feet walking across the floor of the packing room. We heard laughter and chairs scraping, and then voices became fainter. I went to the door and opened it and saw workers going out the rear. It was four o'clock, quitting time in Honolulu. I came back to my chair and sat down.

Lily said, "Tom, where is the mail delivered?"

He jerked his head toward the outer room. "The receptionist gets it. Do you think—"

"Wait a minute," I said excitedly. "We'd better bring you up to date. Lily and I have just come from Blanche's house. And just as we got there . . ."

When I finished telling him Tom said in a hard voice, "So that's the picture. No wonder the girl was so sure of herself. He's paying her to intercept my mail."

He began to pace the floor. The rear door opened and closed again, and then the building felt silent and empty.

Lily said, "Shouldn't the tea be here by now?"

"Of course it should!" Tom was angry with the frustration of a man who wishes to act and doesn't know which way to turn.

"I had better call Hartford Tseng," Lily said, and picked up the phone. Tom looked curiously at her and I realized he knew nothing about Mr. Tseng. I didn't try to explain—there was too much else to consider at the moment.

While Lily spoke in a low voice I joined Tom in his floor pacing. "Webster helps himself to cars when he needs them," I said, remembering the stolen Ford which had killed Yao and the grocery truck he used to reach Blanche's house. "Maybe he has intercepted your delivery."

"He won't get far," Tom threatened. "If that tea isn't delivered within the next half hour I'll have every radio car on this island alerted."

He started out, saying, "I'm going up to see Knight."

One minute later he was back. "The door is locked. He's gone."

"What shall we do now?" I asked.

He looked at his wrist watch. "I said thirty minutes. Then I'm going to call the police. Intercepting a shipment from the tea examiner is federal stuff."

Perhaps fifteen minutes had passed, and Tom was beginning to look like a runner set for a sprint, when we heard a noise in the reception room. He opened the door and saw an Oriental boy with a piece of paper in his hand.

"Ten chests of tea," he said. "I tried the back door but nobody answered."

"Drive around again," Tom said. "I'll be right there."

"The truck's in back now."

We went to the rear of the building where the truck stood at the loading platform with its motor running.

"In here," Tom said, and helped the driver carry in ten matting-wrapped chests identical with those we had seen in New York. Tom signed for the shipment and gave the boy a tip and then looked at us with an expression of half triumph, half puzzlement. He locked the door, then found a pair of heavy scissors and began to cut the matting of a tea chest. He slit the lining of lightweight tin and held the chest up while the tea poured out with a dry little sound. Fragrance met our nostrils as tea covered the table.

But that was all. Just tea.

He brushed it into a huge empty carton and opened the second chest. As he spilled tea again, Lily said, "The substitute chest you sent to our house in New York was different from the others."

Tom stared at her. "Different? How?"

Lily touched one of the chests on the floor. "You see this chop mark? On that chest the chop was identical, but there was a smudge of black paint a few inches below it. Perhaps we can find—"

Tom was already turning over the chests, examining each. At the fifth he stopped. "Like this?"

Lily bent to examine it. "Very much."

He opened that one. Before it was half emptied he said, "This isn't the same tea!"

It was black and the leaves were much smaller and harder than the other leaves. We compared teas. The Dragon Well was lighter in color and contained a few dried flower petals. Although by then we knew it was useless, Tom emptied the rest of the tea chests. Then he stood and looked at the littered table. "They've done it again," he said at last. "Somehow they managed to make a substitution."

He dusted his hands and said, "Well, Miss Wu, what do you suggest we do now?" He couldn't help showing resentment.

Lily sighed. "I don't know. But I should like to sit down."

We went to the front office and the three of us sat and lit cigarettes and stared at each other for a moment, in a depressed silence.

The telephone rang.

Tom picked it up. "Yes? Yes, she's here." He handed the phone to Lily. She listened. She became very still as the speaker continued to pour information in her ear. Watching her, I knew this was important. Gradually Tom caught the tenseness and stared too. Lily set the phone down and turned to us.

"That was Orchid Tseng," she said. "She called from somewhere on Kalanianole Highway in a great hurry. She is following Hollis Knight's station wagon and it is headed around the island. She will call back as soon as she dares stop again."

Both Tom and I had jumped up as she gave us this information. We looked at each other with dismay, thinking that having to sit and wait here for another telephone call was going to be punishment. Lily felt the same way. She called the Tseng house again and got no answer.

"If we could find someone, quickly, who would take a message for us—" she began, and I said, "Steve Dugan! Her office is close. She'll do it, if we can find her."

Steve was there. She agreed to come right over. While we waited Lily said, "There's plenty of gas in the car? Good. Tom, isn't that gun here somewhere?"

"In the tasting room." He went to get it.

Steve arrived in ten minutes. We briefed her rapidly and she sat behind Tom's desk and took off her big shoes and put her feet up. "Okay," she said "Beat it."

As we started out I suggested, "If we go by the Pali road we'll land about midway on the island. Then we can turn in either direction."

"Yes," Lily said, and Tom, who was in the back seat, grunted agreement.

We stopped at a store in Nuuanu to call Tom's office. No news yet. We drove into the valley through deepening evening shadows and mist which began to float from jungled depths between the mountains. Fortunately there was not much traffic and I was able to maintain pretty good speed, although the descent from the Pali seemed interminable.

From another phone Lily called the office again. She came out and said, "Steve heard from Orchid. She followed Hollis Knight's car into a filling station and heard him ask the way to Mokapuu Point. The man who calls himself Webster is with him."

"Where did Orchid call from?"

"I don't know. He is probably going to the cottage."

"Hurry, will you?" Tom said.

Lily took a flashlight from the glove compartment and gave it to Tom. We turned from the highway onto the dirt road which led to the sea. When we were near the house I switched off the lights and Tom got out and walked in front of the car with the flash held low and shaded so that it barely lighted a rut for the left front tire. At the end of the road no other car was visible.

"They are not here yet," Lily said.

"If they're coming here!" I worried. "Now, what will we do with this car?"

"Drive around that big rock," Tom suggested.

I managed to get almost completely past it before the tires hit a boulder. Tom yanked the rug out and laid it over the rear bumper to hide the chrome. If they arrived in a hurry, if they were intent on watching the road, the little car might go unnoticed. At any rate we couldn't dither, for we saw lights approaching. We started down the path to the cottage.

At the seaward side of the house we stopped. Tom said, "We're better off out here." He added in a grim voice, "They'll have to open some windows."

No one made any comment on that.

We stood in darkness. The motor of the other car died, a door slammed. Muffled voices, a curse as someone stumbled, scuffling down the rough path.

"This thing's heavy," Hollis complained. "It weighs twenty pounds."

"Stop whining. That's all you've done for the past two weeks."

They reached the front of the house. The storm door squeaked back. The second door opened and they went inside. A light came on. Then the window near us was thrust open and Hollis said, "Why did you have to insist on a lousy place like this? Christ, it stinks in here!" He opened more windows.

Hollis hadn't been here before. I wondered what he thought had happened to Henry.

"Dead rat somewhere," the other said.

We squeezed together outside and watched.

"Put it on this table," the white-haired man directed.

"Do this. Do that," Hollis growled. "Why can't you carry a few things, take a few chances around here?"

"Shut up, you fool. I told you I've been sick. As for taking chances . . . Here, give me that knife."

Hollis gave it to him. He cut the matting of the chest carefully. "What kind of chest did you use?" he asked.

"It looks exactly like this. When the truck came I hid under the loading platform. It was easy to switch. It wouldn't have been if this had been one of the first they took out."

"That mischance," Webster said, "would have been unfortunate for somebody."

He was using a long-bladed knife. It slipped through the inner lining and he ran the sharp blade carefully around and lifted the tinfoil out whole. He reached into the tea and took out a couple of handfuls which he sifted through his fingers.

"Hey," Hollis said. "Don't throw the stuff around like that. It's hard to clean up."

The other man didn't answer. He was shifting a second double handful of tea. He reached into the chest a third time, and we heard him exclaim with satisfaction. He drew out a strip of brown ribbon about eighteen inches long. It was two pieces of silk glued together. He ran it through his fingers and counted. "Thirty-three!" he said. His hands shook.

"Let me see!" Hollis reached, and the ribbon was jerked from his grasp.

"Wait. We'll count the lot when we get to Blanche's house."

"Isn't it risky? Don't you think she might—"

"Might what? Blanche will do as I tell her. I made sure of that today."

There was a noise at the rear of the house, the sound of rocks sliding. Both men stiffened. "What's that?" Hollis quavered.

"Probably some animal. Why don't you go and see?"

"Me?" His voice grew shrill. "Why the hell should I have to do everything? You go."

Webster put the ribbon in his pocket. He picked up the knife and went into the kitchen, out of our sight. Hollis waited. The other man came back, saying, "Nothing there, of course. But I found something interesting in the pantry. Come and see."

Hollis followed him. We took advantage of the chance to shift position at the window. I whispered, "What are you going to do, Tom?"

"Wait till they come out together." He touched his side pocket where the gun was a sagging bulk.

Hollis didn't come back. Webster appeared, alone, and then proceeded to move hurriedly. He took old magazines from a corner shelf and tore pages from them. He piled these under a wicker chair and tossed its cushions aside. He went to the kitchen again and returned with a can of kerosene from the stove. He poured this on the chair and papers.

"He's going to set the house on fire!" I cried more loudly than I intended. At that sound he turned, stared blindly at the window, then darted into the kitchen. We heard the rear door slam.

By the time we got around the house he was halfway up the rocky slope, climbing incredibly fast, his white hair a moving blur in the night.

A shot rang out. The blur stopped, wavered, and moved on. Another shot and the dim figure jerked, swayed, and tumbled down the hillside in a rush of dirt and rocks.

Then a flashlight went on. Partly revealed behind its beam was a silk-robed massive figure moving toward us.

"I think that he is dead," Mr. Hartford Tseng said. "I am a very accurate shot."

He was dead. In his pocket, when Lily removed the brown silk ribbon of pearls, she found the .bloody knife with which he had killed Hollis. Tom stumbled over Hollis' body when he went into the kitchen. Neither Lily nor I wished to see him.

We drove to the nearest restaurant and had coffee and waited for the police to arrive. Mr. Tseng was not with us. He had gone back to Honolulu, suggesting that we keep him out of the story by saying that Tom had shot in self-defense after the murder of Hollis. He gave Tom his gun, which was not registered. Police would never be able to question Henry about its being in his office.

"They're going to think it very odd that we didn't report Hunter's death," Tom said.

"We didn't know about it," Lily said. "You suspected Hollis Knight of smuggling and followed him tonight when you saw him switch those tea chests. You and Jean have been worried about Henry Hunter. But since his niece had already searched the cottage you did not go to Mokapuu until you trailed the two men here tonight."

"The newspapers are going to make a big deal out of those pearls," I commented.

"Not nearly so much as if we had to tell them the whole story," Lily insisted. "They do not need to know that the pearls came so recently out of China. We can tell them they were stolen from Madame Li in Hong Kong. Mr. Tseng will pay the duty."

"Those pearls," Tom said. "I'd like to have a look at them. Up to now they haven't been real to me."

Lily took the brown strip from her purse and laid it on the table. When she peeled the two pieces of silk apart, the pearls rolled before us. Tom whistled.

"They're very small to be so valuable," he said. "You'll probably have to tear Hunter's house apart to find where that guy hid the rest of them."

"No," Lily said. "I have the others." She brought a knotted handkerchief from her purse. We counted sixty-six pearls.

"Where did you get them?" I asked, although I had already guessed.

"From Blanche's room, of course," she said. "When she produced that story of the identification tag I knew she was lying. If he had been looking for something so small, he would have opened her purse."

"Where were they? In the aquarium?"

"Yes," she said. "Stuffed into the body of the diver. I took them out while Blanche was telephoning the Fentrisses. It was really quite simple."

Tom stood up. "I think that's a police car outside."

As we went out to meet the police I thought of Blanche. I wondered what her face would look like when she discovered that what she had lied and schemed for had been so neatly taken from her. Then

I had to think of grimmer things as we got into the car again to lead the police back to that cottage at Mokapuu Point, where Henry had so recently kept his rendezvous with the Waikiki Widow, and where now three men lay dead.

"And so," Steve Dugan said, and there was slight scorn in her voice, "you sent the jewels of the Empress on to New York?"

Lily smiled at her. She likes Steve. "They may be just excretions of irritated oysters to you. But think of what they mean in money."

"Yeah," Steve said, and wiggled her toes in the grass.

It was two days later. We were in the garden of our Tantalus house, and we had been telling Steve the rest of the story. At our apology for holding some of it back she had shrugged. "Skip it. If all the unprintable news in Hawaii was put into type it world crowd the Congressional Library. I'm just trying to earn an honest buck. I don't want to hurt anybody."

She picked up her glass of iced tea. "This tastes funny without rum."

"Do you want a drink?" I asked.

"It's too hot." She took up our former conversation. "So this guy Donnelly had a very good reason for needing false papers to get back to the United States. He was wanted for murder, eh?"

"That's right," I said. "When they checked his serial number they found that out. He assaulted a fellow officer in China, then killed a guard to escape from prison."

Steve scowled. "Vicious bastard, wasn't he?"

"Reckless and vicious," Lily agreed. "He must have considered himself quite clever for traveling as a missionary. There is almost no doubt that he murdered Matthew Webster for the pearls and his papers. He told Janice that the mission was burned. He liked to use fire." She gave a little shudder.

"So he got shot by Tom Brittain, only it was really Mr. Tseng. How about a feature on the Tseng family?" Steve asked. "Do you think they'd mind?"

"You will have to ask Hartford Tseng," Lily said. She did not mention that he was now on his way to New York with Madame Li's pearls.

Shizu came to the balcony to say someone wanted to see me. I went into the house to find Tom Brittain with a tall, pretty girl at his side whom I had difficulty at first in recognizing as Jean Hunter. She wore a smart dress and high heels and nylons. She also wore lipstick. I decided, as I welcomed them, that Jean's former clothes might have been her rebellion against the conventionality of her family.

"We can't stay," Tom said. "I'm taking Jean to the lawyer to sign some papers."

Probably Henry's estate, I thought. Jean's face sobered as he mentioned this, but there was no horror in her eyes. Jean had not seen her uncle dead.

Tom gave me an odd look. "Have you talked to Blanche yet?"

"No. She's probably keeping quiet for a while." Blanche had been mentioned by the press as a "very good friend" of Henry Hunter and Hollis Knight. We had not disclosed her intimacy with the third man.

Tom gave me another of those looks. "When I stopped by her house a while ago, I found the Fentrisses installed there, very pleased with themselves. They said Blanche had gone to one of the other islands for a rest."

"Oh," I said.

Jean had been admiring the Chinese calligraphy on the wall. She turned and told me, "I'd love to sit and study this for a couple of hours sometime. I'm working on designs for Tom's new packaging."

Tom grinned. "With New York full of artists, I have to come all this way to find someone who understands exactly what I want."

He added, "Remember Mackenzie, the tea-taster? He's on his way here now to take over the Honolulu office. Mac inherited some money from his brother in Scotland, and as soon as the estate is settled, we'll draw up partnership papers."

"He'll love it here," I said.

"He certainly will. No snow." Tom looked at Jean. "Ready?"

They left and I went back to the garden and told Lily and Steve about their call.

"He didn't have to come all the way up here to relay that news item," I said. "He could have telephoned."

"Of course," Lily commented. "But how otherwise could Jean have shown you her new look? It is nice to know that she is so feminine."

"So the Fentrisses are in that fancy house?" Steve got to her feet and muttered something about coming right back. She rejoined us with a big smile on her face. "Had a hunch," she explained. "Just checked the airport and found that a passenger named Mrs. Harry Fentriss left here last night, en route to Detroit."

"After all that act she put on with the passport," I said, "I was sure she'd go to Manila."

"Detroit," Lily said, "had better watch out."

"Uh," Steve said. "I'll bet she got a shock when she looked for those pearls."

The dimple deepened in Lilt's cheek. "Possibly not, if she packed as hurriedly as I think she did. When I went for her powder I bought some substitutes. I broke the string and was careful to put sixty-six pearls back inside the diver."

"Where did you get them?" I demanded. "At a curio store?"

"They were cultured pearls," Lily said, "and rather pretty. They cost seventy-eight dollars."

Steve snorted. "That blond *wahine's* gonna have a helluva jolt when she tries to sell them, wherever she goes."

"Wherever she goes," I echoed, "she's got Gordon's diamond, and the clothes Henry bought for her. Nevertheless, I think we ought to wish her luck. She'll need it."

"Oh yes," Lily said. "I agree with you. Let us do that."

So we smiled, each of us with her private opinion of the lady. Then we raised our iced-tea glasses and drank a toast to the Waikiki Widow.

THE END

The first three Lily Wu/Janice Cameron books have all been reprinted by The Rue Morgue Press: *The Chinese Chop* (0-915230-51-8), *The Kahuna Killer* (0-915230-47-X) and T*he Mamo Murders* (0-915230-51-8).

The Rue Morgue Press reprints vintage mysteries from the 1930s to the 1950s. To suggest titles or to get a catalog of our publications write to The Rue Morgue Press, P.O. Box 4119, Boulder, CO 80306.